WELL

WELL

Matthew McIntosh

Grove Press, New York

"Fishboy" previously appeared in an altered form in *Playboy*.

"Chicken" first appeared in *Ploughshares*.

"Looking Out For Your Own" first appeared in *Puerto del Sol*.

"Grace (So long! part II)" first appeared as "Grace" in a hand-set letterpressed edition of nine copies (state 1) and thirty (state 2), published by Well Known Press.

The phrase "Though occasionally glaring or violent, modern color is on the whole eminently somber" is borrowed wholly out of context from John Ruskin's *Modern Painters III* (1856). Spellings have been Americanized.

The affirmations on pages 31–32 were taken from a now-defunct Web site, which did not name the original sources. Other current sites use similar and often identical affirmations, and likewise don't name sources. I assume they are part of the public domain.

Lyrics on page 32 are from:
PERHAPS LOVE
Words and Music by John Denver
Copyright © 1981 Cherry Lane Music Publishing Company, Inc. (ASCAP)
  and DreamWorks Songs (ASCAP)
Worldwide Rights for DreamWorks Songs Administered by Cherry Lane Music
  Publishing Company, Inc.
International Copyright Secured All Rights Reserved

Published simultaneously in Canada
Printed in the United States of America

FIRST EDITION

Library of Congress Cataloging-in-Publication Data

McIntosh, Matthew.
    Well/Matthew McIntosh.
      p. cm.
    ISBN 0-8021-1751-1
    1. Working class—Fiction. 2. Seattle (Wash.)—Fiction. I. Title.

PS3613.C539W45 2003
8.13'.6—dc21

2002044687

Design by Erin Kincaid and Matthew McIntosh
Set in Adobe Trump Mediaeval and Gill Sans

GROVE PRESS
841 Broadway
New York, NY 10003

03 04 05 06 07 10 9 8 7 6 5 4 3 2 1

for Erin

CONTENTS

IT'S TAKING SO DAMN LONG TO GET HERE (IV)

I struck up a conversation with one of the older guys, a contractor—I'd seen his truck outside, a huge white beast with his name and face painted on the side. We drank and laughed and got to know each other a little. For some reason I asked him if he'd been in the War, Vietnam, and he said, No, I had a high number. I didn't have to worry about that shit, he said. I stayed here and took care of all the pussy...

INTRODUCING...

You didn't know what to say to something like that. But I wasn't surprised. I'd known him since we were kids. I just moved on to the next thing. He was living then in Sea-Tac and wanted to get together sometime—he wanted to start a band—and when it was his stop, he rang the bell and stood up...

ONE MORE

GUNMAN

IT'S TAKING SO DAMN LONG TO GET HERE (V)

Then there was nothing. A dial tone. I'd hung up on her. The first time I called back it went to her voice mail. So I hung up. Then I called right back and it started ringing but then nothing—I thought she answered it but just wasn't going to say anything—you know, the silent treatment. I said, I can hear you. I know you're there. But I couldn't and I didn't...

IT'S TAKING SO DAMN LONG TO GET HERE (VI)

I'm walking out the door and I turn around and I wave bye for some reason, and I don't even know who I'm waving to, I mean I don't know *now*, and I probably didn't know *then*, and one thing I notice as I'm walking away is the lawn could really use some watering because all that's left is practically dirt, and when I walk down the walk, dust and dirt go swirling up in the air around where the grass should be, which is another weird thing...

If I had to try and make some sense out of it I guess I would have to say that I worry I'm going to be waiting so long I'll forget what I'm waiting for. Does that makes sense? You worry you'll forget what you're waiting for and then you worry one day you'll forget that you are waiting for anything at all. Maybe you'll get up one day and go to work, and after work you'll come home and sit down in front of the TV, for instance. Or the radio or whatever. And you turn the volume down because all of a sudden you have the sense that *something's slipped your mind...*

And surely I am with you always,
to the very end of the age.

MATTHEW 28:20

IT'S TAKING SO DAMN LONG TO GET HERE (I)

Maybe not always, but a lot of the time. It doesn't matter where I actually am, it's all the same. For instance, I could be walking to the mailbox or driving in to work and I will get this thing—not a picture but a sort of *perception*, this sort of *sense*, in the same way you imagine the shapes of the walls and the furniture when you're walking through a familiar dark room, that's how it is—and I am always struck with the perception that I'm there, at the bottom of a well. And I've never even *seen* a well that I can remember, except for on TV and in movies, but I've always felt this way. Meaning, I've felt this way about the well since childhood. Or maybe it didn't happen until adolescence, but there I am. I feel that way right now, I really do. I mean, I'm looking into your face right now, but somewhere *deeper*, somewhere behind it all, I could swear that I'm at the bottom of the well. That sounds crazy, doesn't it? My husband tells me I have a constant look of *near-absolute abandonment* on my face. He says I wear that expression all the time.

So I was at the grocery store the other day—this is what I was supposed to be getting at—I'm sorry, I've never been good at getting to the point—I was in line at the grocery store and for some reason I was feeling particularly at ease with myself, and with my situation, the world on this particular day was feeling very adequate, you know, everything was good. For some reason I was looking up at the beams and through the skylight—it was one of those enormous warehouse grocery stores that are springing up all over the place—actually, I think *this* was the reason: I was contemplating all the ways in which the world changes; or not all the ways it changes, but more specifically, I was contemplating this *one particular way* that it was changing. I was focusing on the skylight and I was thinking of a time where it was an unheard of thing to have a skylight in a grocery store, not unheard of in a *bad* sense, just in an *unheard of* sense; it's just that nobody'd thought to do it at the time. Why are grocery stores so *goddamn big* today? Do you know? Are we eating more? Are we all getting fatter? I mean *some* of these places...

Anyway, I guess I was staring up at the skylight—I must have been doing it for a long time—and remember, I'm happy, I really am, I'm having a good day up to this point—and the little thing ringing me up, she all of a sudden stops what she's doing, and she takes hold of my arm, and she says, "Ma'am, are you all right? Do you need me to call someone?"

Do I need her to *call* someone? I didn't know what to say. What would *you* say? Is there a proper way to answer a question like that? It wasn't the question she asked that was so shocking, of course, but that I'd been so damn happy when she'd asked the question. I'd been really happy. I hadn't been that happy in a long time. Jesus, I don't even know what I was so damn happy about, but I was happy. I said I was fine, a little rudely, probably, and I wrote the check and left the store. I drove home and sat out front in the car for probably twenty minutes, until my daughter came out and asked me what I was doing, and how long I was going to stay in there.

BURLESQUE

Adda put down her nail file and lay back on the bed.

Len, saving one last hit in the bottom of the bowl, exhaled, and put the pipe down. Quietly, he walked to the bedroom door, stood outside and listened for her. Then, hearing nothing, he left, shutting the apartment door behind him quietly, then down the hall to the fire escape, down the stairs and through the alley behind the strip club [inside of which the girls were downstairs getting dressed, the bartender was leaning across the bar joking with the DJ, the manager vacuumed the red walk-up carpet, the waitress was beating the dust out of a couch cushion with her fist, the bouncer sat on his stool re-arranging his tie, waiting to hear the word and turn the sign on to say: OPEN], and across the parking lot to the market. He nodded to the old Asian man behind the counter and picked up another six-pack from the cooler. The game had just started and the Asian man was watching it on a small TV behind the counter.

We're not doing so well, Len said, and the Asian man said, No, we are not.

We're not like we used to be.

No, the man said. Not like nineteen ninety-six.

I miss Kemp.

Yes.

That was the team that could have won a championship. We lose tonight we won't even make the playoffs.

But if we do make the playoffs, the man said, I think we will do something special.

Len agreed. In their hearts, they were optimistic people.

They said goodbye and Len walked back towards the apartment with his beer.

Adda was the girl that he wanted: beautiful, smart—smarter than him, though he wouldn't admit it. The best lay he'd ever had. Adda did things to him he could never tell anyone.

Someday he hoped to start his own marble and tile business and marry her and build her a nice house. Retire by forty. A couple rugrats. He wanted to treat her good. He never had much money but he always paid for everything. He paid for the weed, he bought her wine coolers, he took her out and picked up the check. It made him feel good.

But now she'd told him she was leaving in the morning to visit her fiancé in California who wanted her back. She said she owed it to the guy to give him a week.

She'd been with R since she was fifteen and then a few months ago he'd left Federal Way, asking her to come, but she told him she couldn't; she was going to dental hygienist school, she said she wanted to be certified. But that wasn't the real reason—she hated looking into people's mouths and she quit soon after he left, got a job answering phones at a lawyer's office in Seattle. The real reason was it was occurring to her then that she didn't know if she really loved R.

When she'd told Len she was leaving and why, he'd said, You don't owe him nothing.

You don't know what you're talking about.

I don't know what I'm talking about?

You've never been with someone that long. You don't know what it's like.

I don't give a shit what it's like.

At first, when they'd gotten together, Len hadn't cared that she had a fiancé or that the guy had money or that he was taller than Len and better-looking from the picture he'd seen in Adda's wallet. What did it matter to him? What did *she* matter to him back then? He was just fucking some dude's girlfriend. It turned him on. He used to imagine the guy opening the bedroom door while Adda was going down on him, he imagined himself saying something smart like: She insists on doing this after every meal. It didn't matter then. But sometime over the past four months, Adda had turned into *his* girl and he'd started locking the door, not wanting to give her back.

When she told him she was leaving, he'd said, No you're not. I already decided.

You're not going. You're not leaving.

You can't make me not go.

You don't think I can?

No, she'd said. You can't.

Well, why the fuck do you wanna go down there, anyway?

She didn't really know.

Why *was* she going down to California when things up here were fine with Len? She wondered if she really felt she owed R something or if it was just that she wanted to see what his life was like down there. See what kind of life she would have had if she hadn't have stayed.

R had said, Come down and see the house I bought for you.

He's a fag, Len had said.

He's not a fag.

He *is* a fag.

Psychology books and tapes hadn't helped Adda understand why she'd felt so relieved when R had left.

I'm going, she'd said to Len. That's all there is to it.

For how long?

I told you.

One week only?

Yes.

Then you're coming back?

Yes.

Where are you gonna stay?

Where do you think?

You can't stay with him!

She'd said, I don't want to talk about this anymore.

Adda you can't fucking stay with him!

She called Len her Come Machine. He took pride in seeing how many times he could make her come in one go. They had a joke that if he reached six Adda would wash his truck. They fucked everywhere: on the roof and in bathrooms and changing rooms and one time on the stage after her dance class when everyone had gone home and on her boss's desk one night floating high above the city in the dark—it was so beautiful and down below in the dark the red and white lights, the cars slid down the freeway slid down the valley between the dark mountains and the dark warm sea and what was underneath and Len didn't stop. She loved fucking him. They did things she'd never tell anyone.

He'd said, Well, where are you gonna sleep?

Len, just stop it.

You're gonna sleep in his bed with him?

Stop it. I don't want to talk about it anymore.

And they talked to each other during sex and called each other names and she liked it. And he let her be the man sometimes. A woman could be a man as well as a man could. Because a woman knows the difference. When she was with R she'd never thought to do or be anything other than what she was, and who she was then was not anyone special: a girlfriend, a dental-hygienist-in-training.

She didn't care if you brushed. She didn't give a shit about plaque. She never flossed, herself. Her teeth were stained.

Had she loved R then? Did she love Len now? Was it enough to care for a person's well-being? Was it enough to be attached to someone? Enough to desire? Did it make any difference that one could make her come and the other couldn't or that one had a dream that was coming to fruition and the other a dream that he would never fulfill because—well, because she couldn't see it happening?

Was all this—had it always been—was all she capable of—just a cheap imitation of love?

(What are you waiting for, Adda?

I don't know.

What's wrong with you, Adda?)

She didn't know.

Was anyone actually in love?

(*Are any of you out there in love?*)

She could see Len down on the street, walking back to the apartment with a bag in his arms. She could see on the window that it was beginning to rain. He looked so small.

Adda let the curtain fall and sat back down on the bed. She went back to working on her fingernails, looking up every so often at the door.

Len was almost home.

And what if she let that guy touch her? Adda wouldn't say that she wouldn't.

You don't understand, she'd said. You don't know what you're talking about! Then she'd gone into the bedroom and locked the door and he'd stood outside, saying:

Just promise me you won't let him touch you, Adda! That's all I want to hear! Just that you won't let him touch you! You don't have to tell me anything else except that you won't let him touch you! That's all I want to hear! Just that he won't touch you!

Len had never hoped for anything and with her there was hope he could hope for something Christ what if she doesn't come back?

He needed her in the morning before he went to work. He needed her in the evening when he came home, tired. He was lowman all day.

He couldn't even tell you how he needed her.

She ***** ** **** *** ** *** *** **** * *****.

Now he stopped in front of the apartment building, looked up.

(Please don't leave, Adda. Just stay. It makes me crazy. Don't leave, Adda. Stay. Please stay.)

Len sat down on the curb and lit a smoke.

Adda, after counting in her head much more time than it should have taken Len to dial the code to the front door, open it, walk through the lobby, then up the five steps, around the corner, open the door to the stairwell and walk through, then up the two flights of stairs, through the door, then make a right turn, then a left, then down the hall and open the apartment door, got up again from the bed and, lifting the curtain with her fingers, looked down.

Nate thought about it, then hung up the phone and said to his girlfriend, I'll do it later. The game's on.

Do it now! Sammie said.

He picked the phone back up. Began to dial. Looked at the game on in the other room. Hung it up again.

They were coming back. Down by ten now in the second. They'd been down by twenty in the first.

He walked past her and sat back down on the couch, picked his beer up from the coffee table, took a drink. I'll do it later.

I don't want you to do it later! she said. I want you to do it
now!

Game's on, Nate said.

She picked up the phone and slammed it down hard on the
receiver. She did it again.

Good, good, said Nate. Payton grabbed the rebound. Ran up
the court while the defense backpedaled. Lobbed it to Baker,
who blew the dunk. (Fucking Baker.) The ball went flying into
the stands.

Now she was in front of the TV. Are you gonna call or not?
she said.

Not.

You said you would.

Your ass is blocking the screen. Move it.

She didn't move.

Move please.

She turned the TV off.

Hey! Nate said.

You said you were gonna call!

I'll call later! I'm watching the game!

Then give me the number! *I'll* call the bitch!

No, I don't think so.

He wasn't in the mood today. He wasn't patient enough. Get
out of the way. He pointed the remote at her stomach, hit the
button.

You call her right this minute! she said. You tell her if she
ever calls here again I'll kill her! I wanna hear you do it!

Just settle down.

Don't tell me to settle down! I don't want some skank calling my man!

Fine. Now move.

This isn't over!

Fine. Move it or lose it.

She moved and Nate hit the button again and the game came

back on. Sammie stood to the side biting her lip and watching the screen and then she went back into the kitchen and filled the coffeepot. She abruptly put the pot down and walked back into the living room, grabbed the remote from Nate's hand and turned the TV off again.

She thinks she can call here and she can't! You go in there right now and tell her if she calls here again she's dead!

I will! Turn it back on!

I'll turn it back on when you call her and tell her!

I'll call her later! I don't get what the big deal is!

You don't get what the big deal is, huh? She's a *whore!*

She's not a whore.

She is a *whore!*

I wouldn't be calling people whores, Nate said.

Oh really! Now what is that supposed to mean?

Nothing. Gimme the remote! The game's on! For fuck sakes!

Why is she *mysteriously* calling again all of a sudden?

(Sammie you get so crazy and jealous and flip out and I can't reason with you I can't talk to you you just keep going on and on and...)

I told you, Nate said. She was upset.

Well why is she calling *you?* Why doesn't she call one of her little *skank friends?*

Can I just watch the game in peace please? Can I?

What was she so upset about then?

Nothing.

Tell me what she was so upset about!

Jesus Christ...

Tell me why she called!

(Just shut up please. Please just shut up. I'm not in the mood right now. Just leave me alone.)

Tell me!

(Just go into the other room and leave me alone. God, why do you have to be like this?)

You better tell me!

She wants me to go to church with her.

Excuse me?

She's cleaned up and she thinks she wants to save my immortal soul.

Oh, really! Sammie shifted her weight from one leg to the other. Well let me tell you something that bitch couldn't be *cleaned up* with an elephant brush and let me tell you something else your immortal soul doesn't *need* to be saved and if anyone's gonna save it it's gonna be *me!*

Right.

And that bitch cannot call *my house* and talk about *my man's* immortal soul on *my phone!* What did you tell her?

What? I told her no. I told her to leave me alone.

That's not what you told her! You were talking for fifteen minutes!

Nate sighed. Will you please just turn the game on? Will you please just turn the TV on?

I heard you laughing, Nathan. You better not be fucking her!

(Jesus Christ...) I'm not fucking her!

You better not be fucking that little slut!

Quit cursing. You sound like a whore.

Oh, now you're calling me a whore.

Yes, I'm calling you a whore.

You're the whore!

Yeah, I'm the whore, Nate said. I'm the one who puts my tits in their mouths. I'm the one who jerks them through their pants.

Oh really! Sammie said. First of all: *Fuck you!* Second of all:

You like this apartment? You like driving the 4Runner?
You like the weed you smoke? You like that TV?

Forget it, Nate said.

You like the food in the fridge? You like that beer you're
drinking?

Forget it.

You want to get a job? You want to sell your skateboard?
You want to sell your guitars?

Just forget it.

She can't just *go to church!* She's still a *whore!* God doesn't
forget!

Just—(shut up please shut the fuck up)

God won't forget that she's a *whore!*

Just shut up you don't know nothing about it!

God won't—

Just shut the fuck up before I slap you in the face!

Oh, slap me! *Please* slap me! Slap away!

Don't you have to work now? Nate said. Shouldn't you be
licking a pole? Don't you have a dick to—

Sammie threw the remote at Nate's head, but he ducked
and it sailed right over the couch, shattered the glass of a tropi-
cal fish print on the wall. He stood up to take Sammie by the
shoulders, but she threw her arms about and squirmed away,
so he grabbed her again, by the arms this time, and harder so
as not to lose hold of her, and he picked her up [she was kicking at him so he tightened his grip and turned her so his balls
were out of harm's way] and he walked a few steps towards the
kitchen and threw her to the ground. He turned to go back to
the couch, but she ran at him and cheap-shot him in the lower
back, right on the kidney—*hurt* like *hell* and surprised him, he
turned and swung the hard part of his forearm, forgetting to
hold back and

she dropped.

Oh shit! Nate said. Get up! Sammie! You all right? Oh

damn! I'm sorry! You OK? You surprised me. You all right? Shit. Stay there. Don't move. I'm gonna get a towel. Just stay there. Hold on one second.

He went into the kitchen (shit shit shit shit shit shit shit shit shit shit shit shit shit shit shit shit shit shit shit shit shit shit shit shit shit shit shit shit shit shit shit shit shit shit shit shit shit shit shit shit shit), came back with a warm, wet towel. He knelt down and—Let's get you up—gently lifted her to a sitting position, then began wiping her face with the towel, cleaning the blood away from her mouth and chin. Her hair kept falling in the way so he pushed it behind her ears. She looked at him like she didn't know where she was. She rolled her jaw and cupped her lips like a fish.

Are you OK, Sammie? Sammie? Do you know where you are? What year is it?

Ow, she said. She put her hand to her mouth. She touched a bottom tooth and it moved. Ow, she said. Then she started to cry.

Don't cry, Sammie. Don't cry. Don't cry. No, yeah, that's OK. You can cry if you want.

Crying, she put her face down and covered it with her hands. Her hair came loose from behind her ears and covered her the rest of the way.

* * *INTERMISSION * * *

I was the man. I made seven hundred dollars a week and over there that's serious money. You can get your dick sucked for ten dollars and that's a quality whore. You can get whatever you want. I bought the virginity of a beautiful fourteen-year-old girl for two hundred dollars.

My wife won't fuck me anymore. She doesn't like me. She

hates that I brought her all the way over here even though it was her idea. She hates that she married me. She came from a good family. They wanted her to marry an American. They're all whores over there. Even if they're not selling their pussies. She came to America to have the American Dream and now she sees it for what it is. You know where my wife works? She works at Wal-Mart. Selling cameras. When she's not working, she's in the bedroom, asleep, trying to find that dream.

I can't stand my wife. I like my son. He's five. He's very intelligent for his age. He draws beautifully. He's going to grow up to be a famous artist. My daughter...oh, she's beautiful. She's only seven now. She's going to grow up and then I'll be in trouble. Anglo-Asian women are the finest around. I'm going to be in trouble. Yeah, I'm gonna be in some serious trouble then.

They got whatever you want over there. Say you're into opium. Heroin. Whatever. I was never into that shit myself, but it's there. I say that's the *real* land of opportunity. I would have stayed if I could. I had a good job, a nice place. People respected me. Beautiful women. The place I have now is a piece of shit.

I have some marijuana at the house if you want to smoke later. It really wipes you out. I rarely smoke it. I've had it for a long time. The black guy I got it from isn't around anymore. I think he's in jail. I met him at a bar one night and we hit it off. We smoked in the bathroom and then we went to his place. He was living in the basement of an old house and this girl was sitting on a mattress, strung out. She was a rail. She looked awful. I thought I recognized her and a long time later I remembered where I had seen her before. She worked years before at a Mexican restaurant that isn't around anymore. She was the hostess and I'd always wanted to ask her out on a date. I was just a young buck like you. I'd had an interest in her for a long time—I'd even told my pals about her. She was *just beautiful.* She seemed incredibly fresh and clean. I almost asked her out on a date one time. I found out what time she was getting off and then I went in there right at ten and waited for her by the front desk and she came out talking to a man, who happened to be a lot more beautiful than I was, but anyway, I kept waiting for her to finish with him so I could ask her, and I was getting more and more nervous all the time, fidgeting around and the man said something that made her laugh and I knew from the way she laughed that I didn't have a chance and I turned around and walked out. But there she was—although I didn't recognize her at the time—and the black guy asked me if I wanted to fuck her.

You know where I work? I work at St Francis Hospital. Accounts department, doing data entry. I used to make forty thousand US dollars when I was living in Thailand. I worked for an English language newspaper in Phuket town. Forty grand in Phuket, that's like being a millionaire. I could do whatever I wanted, I could have whatever I wanted.

My wife got ovarian cancer and she talked me into quitting my job and coming back to America. She's fine now although sometimes I wish...

She would have had fine treatment in Thailand anyway and I'd still be getting laid. I'm not bitter about it.

My wife used to get upset when I looked at porn on the Internet. Now she just leaves me alone. They have anything a guy could want, but it's not the same.

You know that place, XTC TAN, over on Pac-Highway? It's a tanning place and they do lingerie shows. Well that was just a front. The place used to be a whorehouse. Seriously. Right here in Federal Way. I found out about it after it got closed down. The cops came and shut it down. Now it's under new management. They won't even lay a finger on you.

You know how long it's been since I've been laid? You know how long it's been since a woman has even *touched* my privates?

They do whatever you want over there. You could ask them

to do some weird shit and they wouldn't judge you.

I fucked her. This was about a year ago probably. I gave the black guy another forty bucks and he went into the other room and I went over to the girl on the mattress and got on top of her. I didn't remember who she was. But she just laid there like a dead fish and I pulled her shorts down and went for it and she looked bored. I looked in her eyes and she was looking out the window and she looked so bored.

They never looked bored over there. They always wanted it. They really did. You could look in their eyes and you knew they really wanted it. That's the difference. They know not to lie. They never lie to you over there. I could come.

The redhead was laughing with the girl next to her. She had the most perfectly straight white teeth. Raymond had never seen such perfect teeth. He supposed they might have been bleached. Did they still bleach teeth? Hadn't he read it was bad for the enamel? Maybe they looked so white because she was so tan. Gold top, green shorts. Her top covered her breasts and shoulders. It exposed almost all of her chest and her entire stomach. Even sitting down her stomach looked toned. She must do sit-ups. And her legs! Golden brown. They looked smooth. You'd think a redhead wouldn't tan that well, but—

What are you looking at? his wife said.

The game.

Can you see their faces?

Yeah.

Let me try.

Raymond handed the binoculars to his wife. The crowd cheered loudly. The man to his right knocked his knee against Raymond's. Someone had been fouled. He looked down at the redhead. From up here without the glasses you could barely see anything. You couldn't tell she was so beautiful, so perfect. He guessed that everyone seated this high must just assume that about her and the rest of them. Well, none of the others were anything close.

Let me see them again, he said.

Just a minute, his wife said. Wow, you really *can* see everything! She dropped the binoculars to her lap and turned to him—You can see their lips move, she said, and put them to her eyes again.

Raymond looked at his wife and sighed. She'd never looked anything like the redhead, not even close, but there had been a time... He guessed he couldn't fault her for aging. He couldn't fault her for having kids, menopause. Still, he wished she'd go to the gym, try to work off some of that extra padding, try to get at least *some* of what she'd had back, as much as possible, maybe dye her hair a new color. Wear some tighter outfits. Squeeze that extra weight in. Look at her. She was always wearing those baggy basketball T-shirts. And what kind of a woman wears a baseball cap? The next time he made love to her he would remember the redhead.

The whistle blew. The announcer said: Timeout SuperSonics. There were only a few seconds left in the third quarter.

All right. My turn. Let me see. Raymond grabbed the glasses from his wife's hand as the redhead hopped her way onto the court along with the other girls. A song was playing on the sound system that he faintly recalled hearing somewhere, possibly blasting from behind his daughter's door. He focused on the redhead. She had a great smile, perfect teeth. Her hair couldn't be that curly naturally, could it? Maybe she had it permed. Wouldn't it be something to walk into a barbershop and see her in the chair getting a perm? Wow, she had great rhythm. She bounced up and down to the music, running in place, kicking her legs up high behind her. She clapped her hands above her head. Her breasts bobbed in tandem, barely restrained by the tight fabric of her shirt; they seemed to be smiling too. And those legs... He imagined rubbing his dick along one. She was lying on her side on his down comforter. She was wearing that outfit, smiling. One breast had popped out and she held it in her hand, twiddling the nipple between two fingers. First he felt her leg with his hand and then he rubbed his face up her thigh and then it became too much for him and he just had to whip it out and rub it across her lustrous, silky—

What the hell are you doing? His wife grabbed at the binoculars—Put those away!—knocking him on the side of the nose.

Ow! he said. What?

Don't be a pervert!

What? His right eye began to tear up from the blow.

God! And right in front of all these people! Shameless!

What are you talking about?

You were staring at those girls!

I wasn't staring at *them!* I thought I saw someone I recognized down there. I was trying to see if it was him.

Right.

I was! It wasn't him although it looked like him. He cleared his throat. You thought I was staring at those girls? He chuckled, cleared his throat again. I can see how it might have looked that way, but believe me... He rubbed his nose. Geez, that really hurt.

She appeared to not want to hear it.

Raymond had first seen her back at college and he set about recollecting that now. She'd been sitting under a tree reading a book. She was so beautiful... What was it that had attracted him to her? The backlighting of the sun that set her hair aglow? The wind blowing it across her face, the way she'd gently sweep it out of her eyes with two fingers, turning the page, that forlorn expression on her face?

Was this how it really had been? Or had he seen it in a movie?

Now that he thought about it he was pretty sure he'd seen it in a movie. That's what it was—Catherine Deneuve. They'd gone to a Catherine Deneuve movie on one of their first dates. The story had made his wife cry and afterwards when she had wanted to discuss it, he couldn't remember anything about the movie because he'd been awestruck by Catherine Deneuve, he'd watched her the entire movie without listening or paying any attention to what was happening around her. When she wasn't in a scene, he'd be thinking about her in the previous scene, recalling a particular image, then freezing it in his brain so that he would be able to call it up later. His wife had long straight hair then and she looked a little like Catherine Deneuve; around the mouth, maybe. Where *had* he first seen her? When was it? Could he even remember?

Then a sound like a tsunami crashing and when Raymond looked up, he saw that everyone had jumped from their seats, including his wife. He stood too and reached for her—he had to shout over the din of the crowd:

WHAT HAPPENED?

She was whistling through her fingers.

WHAT HAPPENED? I MISSED IT! WHAT HAPPENED?

WE HIT A THREE-POINTER AT THE BUZZER!

His wife was beaming, clapping her hands to the music coming from the PA, bouncing on her toes, exuberant. She put her arm around him and planted a long kiss on his cheek, and he bounced along with her. The cheerleaders ran onto the floor to lead the crowd in exaltation. Without the binoculars he couldn't see her very well but he remembered...

WE'RE COMING BACK! his wife said. I THINK WE'RE GOING TO WIN! I CAN FEEL IT!

Mr So sighed. It was over. He leaned forward and turned the channel. The bell rang and one of the girls from next door came in and pulled a packet of No-Doz from the box on the counter, slapped it down.

I'm in a hurry, she said.

She said, Hello? English? *Speak—ee Eng—lish? Her—o? Can—you—hear—me—I—don't—have—for—e—ver!*

Mr So stood up. He took her seventy-five cents. The bell rang as she hurried out into the rain. There was nothing special about today.

Len turned off the TV. Fucking shit.

Not to mention Adda was still inside.

He got up from the couch and went over to the door. He said, Goddamnit, when are you gonna come out?

He could hear her turning the pages of a magazine on the other side.

I wanna talk about it some more, he said.

I don't *want*...to talk about it...anymore, Adda said.

Len was tired. (You need to put a stop to this shit right now, man. She was never gonna stay with you anyway. Why the fuck would she stay with you? What do you got? *Dick.* You got *dick.* All she ever wanted was to use you.

Be a man, Len. Be a fucking MAN for once.)

Open the door! he said.

No. Calm down.

Open the goddamn door! He banged on it.

Why don't you go out for awhile, Adda said. Go get a beer. You need to calm down.

You can fuck that fucker for all I care! Len shouted, pulling hard against the door. Fuck him! I don't give a shit!

On second thought, maybe go get yourself a cup of coffee, Adda said. You're drunk.

I'm not going *anywhere!* Open the door! I wanna talk!

Adda turned the page.

Say something goddamnit!

She lay back on the bed. She felt so sorry for him. (I'm sorry, Len. I'm so sorry. I don't know what to do.)

Fucking say something! Len shouted.

Adda cleared her throat.

You're just a fucking bitch, you know that? Len said. You're a fucking bitch! You think you know but you don't know shit! You're just a fucking—

Adda sang:

Thank you! Good—night!

I don't give a shit about you, bitch! I don't give a shit about you!

Sang:

Thank you! Good—night!

Get out of my apartment!

Thank you! Good—night!

Go home!

Thank you! Good—night!

Go back home!

Thank you! Good—night!

Go to California, bitch! he said. Let him put his fucking hands all over you! All over your **** and *** and ***** and let him **** you in the ***!

Thank you! she sang. *Good—night!*
Thank you! Good—night!
Good—night! Good—night!
Good—night!

In his dream, Nate was standing over an enormous fishtank, pissing, but no matter how long he stood there, he would not be relieved. He pissed for what seemed like hours and then he opened his eyes. It was dark. They'd fallen asleep. Jesus, he'd missed the game. He rolled Sammie off his shoulder, stood up naked, leaned back down and pulled the blanket over her tits. She stirred but didn't wake. Her bottom lip was fat and in the dark he could make out a bruise on the side of her mouth. She'd have to see a dentist, maybe call in sick tonight. He had a sudden urge to kiss her softly but instead he walked down the hall to the bathroom and stood over the toilet and sighed and pissed and the goddamn hole in his dick was closed up after the screw and with the first burst came two sideways streams— one that hit his left leg and the other, the new shower curtain Sammie had put up—Damnit!—he stopped quickly and, holding it in, wiped his leg off with toilet paper, wiped the toilet seat down, sat and pissed into the bowl. Relief. Then he flushed, walked back into the living room, put his boxers on, picked up the remote, sat on the edge of the couch by Sammie's head, and hit the button. He felt her put her hand against his back. The TV made a soft popping noise and with a quick flash of blue, the picture came on. Nate picked up Sammie's Percocet vial and swallowed a few down dry. Flicked through the channels looking for a sports wrap-up but couldn't find one. He regretted not reminding Sammie about the cable bill. If the cable was still on he'd know who won the game. He stopped on the news, resigned to waiting.

Who did he think had won? *His* team? If he was a betting man, would he have put money on it? Could he forget the disappointments of past seasons? Could he believe that they had risen to the occasion and won the game? Could he believe that they had not let him down?

You know what I drive? I drive a minivan. I bought it last year. I got it with thirty thousand miles on it. If you would have asked me when I was your age if I'd be my age driving a mini-van with a bitch wife and two kids I'd have said you were crazy. I believed in my *Purpose*, my *Destiny*. I haven't the foggiest idea how to get back up and running again. Maybe leave them some night late and go back to Southeast Asia.

God, it's so beautiful there. You haven't seen a sunset until you've seen those cliffs glowing orange when the sun is almost down, and the ocean, and then as if in a dance a flock of birds rises up from the water and turns and falls and floats and is about to break apart and each bird is caught by the same force and the entire flock turns and falls and floats and each time it looks like they're all going to break apart again, together they turn and fall and float—

I would take a girl on a cruise and we would ride and drink from a flask and watch the sunset, the swollen orange sun over the water, I'd get the whole boat going in a song more than fifty people and we would laugh and sing all of us—*All together now!*—we would drink from the flask and she and I would hold each other.

It was like the movies,

except I don't know any of these people and she's only holding me because I'm paying her to hold me and no matter how hard I try to forget that fact I just can't and my wife is at home wrapping my dinner in Saran Wrap and she's hoping I've just lost track of time again: He's always losing track of time again.

What time is it now, anyway? Do you know? It's dark out, isn't it. I should be going.

There's always next year, Raymond said, and his wife in the passenger seat sighed, staring out the window. She'd taken off her Sonics cap and now held it in her lap. They were in bumper-to-bumper traffic, everyone trying to merge onto the freeway, having trouble in the rain. It always took so long to get back after a game. He'd wanted to stay in the arena until everyone had left, but she'd wanted to leave right away. She was despondent and he wanted to do something for her. But he didn't know what. He loved her greatly. He loved her more than anything in the world. But there were things—too many things—that he *wanted*, and that desire—he couldn't get it out of him. He understood that it occupied much too large a part of himself and it was a part that he could not share with her and because of that they could never really know each other as deeply as they should, she could never know him as deeply as she deserved. But that part—how do you give it up? Who do you give it to? In wonderment, Raymond began to think of the redheaded cheerleader, the way she had smiled, the way she'd moved her body as she had danced a number near the end of the game, each step a short, controlled spasm—he wondered if she became filled with sexual energy when she danced, if she became wet—she must be taking a shower right now, he thought, soaping her body, running the bar of soap down her arms, over and around her breasts, across her belly, between her legs, around her backside, between her cheeks, leaning back in a cloud of steam her hands stroking her face beneath the white-blue stream of water which dripped from and ran from her silky hair her legs her skin...

His wife said, I really thought we were going to win. I thought we had it this time.

I know.

It's just—you get your hopes up.

Yes.

You get your damn hopes up.

Well, Raymond said, there's always next year. He turned to her and smiled. Might as well look on the bright side of things.

She kept staring out the window.

Thank you, Raymond, she said. You're too kind. You're far too kind.

* * * ENCORE * * *

(Head back. Good. You look fine. Get that—wipe that—off.
Deep breath. And...let it out. I know. Don't worry. Smile.)
 I don't want to smile.
(You know what they say: When life hands you lemons, you
go out there and make a big pitcher of lemonade.)
 I don't even like lemonade. I need braces. I look ugly.
(You look fine.)
Jesus, I look a hundred years old.
(You're fine.)
 I don't feel fine.
(You *are* fine. You just have to remind yourself.)
 God, I hate my nipples.
(There's nothing wrong with your nipples. Here. Do
your affirmations. There's nobody in here. Check the stalls.
Nobody.)

 I am a happy, healthy, wholesome, beautiful, positive,
  prosperous person.
 I am extremely well-liked and pleasing.
 I have complete and unconditional worth as a person
  in this universe.
 I accept and acknowledge unconditionally my individuality
  and unique personality.
 I am highly creative, intelligent, attractive, energetic, sexy,
  witty, smart, healthy, and wise.

(OK. Now love.)

 I love myself unconditionally just as I am.
 I give and receive love easily and joyfully.

I always have an abundant supply of love within me.
I radiate love to all persons and places and things that I
    contact each day.
People are just waiting to love me and I let them love me
    abundantly.

(Now the poem. Do it without crying.)

Perhaps love is like a resting place
A shelter from the storm
It exists to give you comfort
It is there to keep you warm
And in those times of trouble
When you are most alone
The memory of love will bring you home.

(Feel better?)

No. I look like crap. No matter what I do I still look like this.
How did I get like this? When did this happen? Jesus Christ.
    (Relax. Your mascara will run.)
    I don't care if it runs.
    (You'll only make things worse. You'll get blue drops all
over your outfit. Just relax. You've got to go out there and put
on a show.)
    I don't want to go out there.
    (Yes, you do. You want to go out there and show them what
you've got. It's your time.)
    I look terrible.
    (No you don't.)
    Yes I do. I look so ugly I want to be sick.
    (Take another hit.)
    God, I'm so ugly...
    ...I'm so fucking ugly.

(There. Wipe that off. Good.)
Why am I like this? What the hell is wrong with me?
(Nothing.)
No, something is. Something definitely is.
(You're fine.)
No. I'm not well. I'm not well.
(You're well.)
I feel so damn alone.
(Admitting you're alone is half the battle.)
That doesn't even make sense.
(You're a star.)
I don't even remember what song I said.
(Yes you do.)
No, I don't. I really don't remember.
(What do you mean, you don't remember?)
Shit, I don't remember the routine!
(How could you not remember?)
I don't remember what I'm supposed to do!
(What are you, a retard?)
Oh, man! I can't go out there! I gotta tell Terry I can't do it!
Oh shit! I'm retarded! What am I gonna do? What the hell am
I gonna do? Oh fuck, I can't remember! What the fuck is it? I
don't remember anything!
(Hopeless.)
Oh Jesus help me! Help me Christ! I can't go out there!
(Just hopeless…)

One night, after he'd added everything up, Jim had come home
with almost fifty dollars and a camera. He'd sold the camera
for twenty bucks to a friend of his, so the grand total that night
had been close to seventy bucks. That had been a good night.
Most nights he only found a few dollars here or there. Sometimes earrings or a wallet, once in awhile a watch. Tonight

he hadn't found a dime. And so he had stopped looking. He'd stopped looking at what he swept up, stopped looking into the trash can after he dumped the pan, stopped rooting through the ticket stubs and napkins and cups and wrappers for money or a check or credit card that might have slipped out of somebody's wallet. It felt to him tonight, the way his luck was going, that he should go home with nothing, so he stopped looking.

Julie was lying on the couch when he got home. The TV was on. She'd ordered a pizza.

Jim thought, We can't afford pizza. Why doesn't she make herself a sandwich! She always wants expensive food!

Have a slice, Julie said. She sat up, then heaved her enormous body over to the next cushion so Jim could sit down. She was due anytime now.

Jim sat and took a piece. Cold and waxy. He put his feet up on the table, one on each side of the pizza box.

That's not very sanitary, Julie said. And you know you should wash your hands.

I washed them at work.

You'll have to wash your hands before you touch the baby. She hit MUTE on the remote. I heard about the game, she said.

Yep.

Too bad.

Too bad.

They almost came back?

They never come back, do they. Not all the way. Did you feed the fish? he said.

I forgot.

Did you clean the tank at least?

I forgot that too. Do you wanna feel? she said. He's kicking.

Do I have to wash my hands first?

Very funny, Mr Comedian.

He wiped his hand on his work pants and placed it on Julie's stomach, and she put her hand over his and pressed down. First he didn't feel anything at all. He thought, I can't feel it. It isn't there. There's nothing there but air. But then he felt it knock. Three times. He thought, There it is. It's real all right.

Julie said, You feel?

Yep.

Isn't it awesome?

Yes.

Aren't you excited?

Jim took his hand back.

He said, I had to cover Randy's section tonight. That's why I'm so late if you were wondering.

He didn't show up?

Bob said he fell off the wagon. Said it was because he was so nervous about the game. They'll probably fire him.

There's a real fan for you.

He's a jackass.

You think they'll really fire him?

I hope so.

We should have him over for dinner.

He eats too much already. He's a fatass.

He eats terribly. He doesn't have anyone to cook for him. All he eats is fast food.

Let him starve.

That's a wonderful thing to say.

The fat fucker can starve.

Very nice, she said.

Jim looked around. He thought, This goddamn shithole... It had once been a sleazy motel run by a couple Arabs. You couldn't drink the water. The heat never worked. The walls were thin and if the neighbors weren't screaming at each other, they were fucking each other with bullhorns. The toilet was always overflowing...

You wanna go to bed? Julie said. I'm so tired.

Some asshole wiped shit all over one of his stalls, Jim said.

What? Whose stalls?

His. Randy's. At work.

And you had to clean it up?

Who else? Not Randy.

Disgusting. I hope you washed your hands.

All over: the walls, the floor, the door, the toilet paper, the seat...

Disgusting.

Why the hell would you do that? I don't get what makes a person do that.

A sick mind, Julie said.

Don't they know somebody's gotta clean it up?

Julie rested her head on his shoulder. Jim remembered well. It smelled like shit, he said.

Don't talk about it anymore.

I should have just left it there.

You should have.

I should have just walked out.

You should have just left it.

I couldn't just leave it, Jim said. It smelled so bad...

Quit talking about it. You make yourself feel worse. Why don't you go take a shower? You might feel better.

I won't feel better.

You might.

I won't. I won't feel better. It smelled so bad.

He hadn't known where to start but he'd started on the floor using an industrial strength cleanser and a mop and a bucket and gloves and another bucket and the mop had just smeared it around and the water had turned brown and when he'd finally gotten the floor cleaned there was still so much more to go.

Jim, please. Let's talk about something else.

That fat fucker can starve as far as I'm concerned.

You're right. We won't invite him.

He's not such a fan. He doesn't even know who Jack Sikma
is. *I'm a fan.*

I know you are, Julie said.

Why do you think I took that fucking job in the first place?
Because I like cleaning up shit?

I know, I know.

I'm a fucking fan.

I know you are. *Shhhh.* She rubbed his arm.

Ninety six ninety seven Pacific division champs ninety
five ninety six Pacific division champs ninety five ninety six
Western Conference champs

> *Shhhh*

ninety three ninety four Pacific division champs seventy
eight seventy nine Pacific division champs seventy eight seventy nine

> *shhhh*

Western Conference champs seventy eight seventy nine
NBA champions.

> *shhhh.*

Julie reached to put her hand on Jim's head, but he stood
quickly and walked to the front door.

Jimmy, sit back down, she said. Baby, come sit with me.

He needed some air.

Put your head on my lap.

I'll be back, he said.

Come sit with me. Come here. Lay down.

But he was already through the door. He closed it behind
him and pulled out a smoke, lit it. He leaned over the railing
and looked down into the parking lot.

The rain had stopped. It was quiet. No cars out. But it was
very late and not many people were even awake. The strip
club across the street was closed and all the lights were out.

> *[If only they'd won...]*

One night, he'd lain in bed awake long after Julie had fallen asleep, and he'd gotten up and had dressed quietly and slipped outside, down the stairs, and across the street. He'd walked through the parking lot and gone inside, paid the five-dollar cover, bought a drink, and took a table towards the back. He shook off a girl who petted him and stroked his arm—*You wanna dance?*—and then she had floated away through the smoke and it was dark inside but warm and the music was thick and slow and a pedal steel guitar cried out and he felt tired and worn-through. She left him alone with the girl onstage.

She stood at the rear of the stage with her back to him in a simple white G-string, facing a mirror, swaying slowly to the music. She unfastened her bra in the back and slid the straps down off her shoulders and, still holding on to the front with one hand, she turned her head and looked at him. Slowly danced to the pole, reached for it with her free hand and swung around to the front of the stage—all in perfect rhythm—pulled her hand away and let the bra drop to the floor. She ran her fingers over her breasts, smiling, let go, and took the pole in her hands. She slid down, opening her legs, and rolled onto her back. Touched her breasts and smiled. Looking at him, she stretched for a spray bottle that one of the other girls had brought out to her—sprayed it over her breasts and belly, rolled over onto her stomach and reached behind her, smiling, sprayed it on her ass, between her legs. She rolled again and sprayed it in the air and the cloud descended upon her, she set the bottle down and rolled and he saw that there was glitter and confetti on the stage. It stuck to her as she rolled. She stopped rolling and smiled. On her back, she reached down between her legs and smiled. *Glimmering and shining beneath the overhead lights.* Then someone hit a switch and the black lights came on and Jim saw that her skin was scales and it glowed a cold moonlit underwater blue and then, smiling at him, she slowly ran both hands down her breasts, over her ribcage, down her belly, the

seam of her, then across to her thighs (many of the scales falling off as she touched them with her hands), around to her hips
and hooking her thumbs around both sides of her G-string, she
lifted her pelvis from the floor, and pulled. Lying there on the
stage beneath the black lights, covered in scales, pulling her
panties down (Jim stopped looking), she said, RELIEF—

and he remembered all of this later when he was back
home in bed, trying not to shake the mattress too much and
wake his girlfriend, his eyes closed tight in concentration—he
remembered and—when he finally came to the finale where
she sprayed herself and rolled and smiled and began to pull—

it came, he opened his eyes, he sighed.

She said, *Thank you for coming*, and swam away.

The market was still open.

So he threw his cigarette over the railing and walked down
the stairs, through the parking lot and towards the store [inside
of which the old man was sweeping the floor behind the counter in a rush to get home, then stopped because through the
window he saw a man standing on the median in the middle
of the highway, waiting for a car to pass, which passed, and the
man continued crossing, stepped up onto the curb, and the old
man, who had counted out the register already, realized that
he'd forgotten to turn the sign off and lock the door, so quickly
he set the broom aside and lifted the countertop, hurried to the
door and threw the bolt—the man kept coming, not noticing.
Mr So hurried back behind the counter.

Fingering the chain below the red neon OPEN sign, he........
......pulled it] not noticing that it was closed.

IT'S TAKING SO DAMN LONG TO GET HERE (II)

We had this thing where I'd be Russia and she'd be the States and she'd put on her blue bathing suit top and her red bottoms—and I'd put on this red cape and this pair of yellow boxers—we'd both be really loaded by this point—we'd be mixing our chemicals let's just say—and usually if we could afford it I'd have to be drinking vodka—and we'd sit there watching Wheel of Fortune unless it was Sunday but we never did it on Sunday—and now that I think about it I don't think we ever did it before seven o'clock—because it always started with Wheel of Fortune—but we'd dress up and sit on the couch—or I'd sit on the couch and she'd sit on the floor with her head by my crotch and we'd continue to get plastered—and this girl would always solve the puzzles before me or before anyone on the show except she had trouble with this one guy who was always getting them after one or two letters and consequently not winning much dough—but we'd watch Wheel and after Wheel we'd watch Jeopardy which again she was much better at than me—and I have a huge tolerance but I'm talking about crack cocaine and straight shot after shot—she'd make herself orange and lime cocktails with paper

umbrellas—so we'd be over the moon—and after Jeopardy we'd
watch the prime-time lineup—usually NBC because she likes
their sitcoms better—so maybe like four of those sitcoms and
it'd be like ten o'clock—and if I'm still sober enough to do it
and if I haven't puked all over myself or passed out or overdosed—if all of these things are a Go—after ER or whatever
drama came on at ten she'd turn around and blink her eyes and
she'd put on this old pair of Captain America sunglasses and
she'd go, "Nuke me, baby." This would be around eleven.

MODERN COLOR /
MODERN LOVE

I. He had a car and a job and a nice apartment and he met a girl one night when he was feeling particularly in the vibe and she was in the vibe herself and she had a car and an apartment and no job but she was looking and they hooked up and started spending all their time together and he promised to find her a job in the office where he worked but she didn't really want to work no what she wanted was to move in with him and he was an asshole and he knew that and he didn't like what he'd done with his life and he was going to rectify the crimes against women he had committed and there were a ton of them in thirty-two years and believe him this girl really understood his deeper parts like no one had like no one ever wanted to so when she ran out of money he gave her some and then he moved her in and when her car broke down he took care of it and all she wanted to do was sit around eating Nilla Wafers and all his buddies hated her and when they wanted to go out with him and get loaded she always said no and he was a little embarrassed but not really because look at the tail on that bitch and I can always…

II. On Friday and Saturday nights Shelly and her girlfriends would cruise around in her car, through the Sea-Tac mall parking lot, across 320th, and up through the parking lot of the Old Navy. Shelly had lots of friends and they would smoke cigarettes and play their music with the windows rolled down and park and talk to guys. They would drive to Taco Bell and see who was there and talk to the people they knew or had seen around. They would do whatever drugs they could get their hands on. Getting high was important. Often, because there was never anything real ever going on in Federal Way, they would drive to Seattle and talk their way into the dance clubs, sometimes going home with older guys.

Shelly lived with her mother in an apartment off of west 320th. Her mother ran a take-out teriyaki place eighteen hours a day and never came home until very late. Shelly's friends would always meet at her apartment and drink and smoke weed and do whatever else anyone had. Sometimes things would get out of hand. Once a couple guys she knew had taken a girlfriend of Shelly's into her mother's bedroom after the girl had passed out. Shelly was sprawled out on the couch, barely awake herself, when it happened. She could hear it happening and she was angry, but she was tired. She gave the guys hell the next day and her girlfriend stopped talking to her. Shelly really didn't mind and soon the guys were back at her house and her girlfriend was back with the rest of them and everything was like it always was.

Shelly didn't like her friends much but she needed them. She didn't like the idea of being alone and without these friends of hers she was afraid she wouldn't be anyone. Sometimes a guy would come over and they'd fuck. She liked that. She also liked getting high. Her favorite was crystal methamphetamine. When she was on crystal she thought she was stronger and smarter and better than when she was straight, and she was never tired. She liked that her apartment was the apartment where everyone always met, and she didn't like being by herself.

Shelly wasn't any good at school. She only showed up when none of her friends came to her apartment. Once the principal called Shelly and her mother in to see him, but her mother was tired and didn't speak much English, she couldn't figure out what was going on, and on the way home Shelly explained to her mother in Korean that everyone's parents were being invited down to meet the principal that month, that this is what they do in America, and after awhile her mother gave in and believed her. The next day, the principal told Shelly she was being transferred to the alternative school by the freeway. He grabbed her by the shoulder and said he hoped she would get her act together and quit fucking around.

The alternative school had been called Continuation. A few months before Shelly's name was on the roll, it was renamed Harry S Truman High. She went to Truman a few times and didn't like it. Most of the kids there were lowlifes; niggers and white trash. It could have been useful in scoring drugs, but Shelly knew where to get whatever she wanted. She stopped going and since she was almost seventeen the State couldn't do anything about it. She dropped out and figured she would get her GED later, when she felt like it, go to the University and get a degree in communications.

She stayed out late most nights. When no one was around, she'd go down to the Trolley, an old beer dive across from the new Blockbuster and drink and talk to guys there and go out back and smoke crystal or opium or whatever anyone had and sometimes she'd feel like fucking, so she'd go out to their cars with them or back to their apartments. Most of these guys were lowlifes but she didn't mind so much. Once she woke up in a dark place with a man on top of her and didn't know where she was. She kicked the man off and pulled up her underwear and stumbled in the dark for the door. She opened the door and stepped outside. She was in a parking lot somewhere and there were trees and a field and goal posts and she didn't know where she was, but she knew she was far away. She could see the red sky over Federal Way and she figured she was somewhere to the north. She got back in and told the man to take her to her car. She told him to wait around in case it wouldn't start.

She liked the bars better than driving around and most of her friends couldn't get into bars and most of her friends had become boring as hell anyway. She knew they talked about her behind her back and once she had pulled a knife on a girlfriend of hers and her friends had all left and when they were driving away, one of them threw a rock through the window of her car. No one was coming by her house anymore but she liked it better that way and didn't miss them. Coming home from the Trolley one night, she fell asleep and crossed 320th and drove through a fence and into someone's backyard. She went to jail for the night and in the morning her mother came to pick her up. Her mother wept and said that Shelly had finally become a Real American Whore, that Shelly wasn't her daughter anymore and that she hadn't been for a long time. Shelly really didn't give a shit. She was tired and she wanted a shower and her head and her stomach and her face and her fingers were killing her and it depressed her that she would have to wait until the bars opened at eleven to get a fix.

A man at the Trolley bought her drinks one night and Shelly danced with him in front of the jukebox to some old hippie song she'd always hated and she went to his house with him and stayed there. He was a lot older than her and his house was a piece of shit, but he always had money. Sometimes they would ride around in his red Corvette. A few times, early on, they had gone down to Auburn where he knew some people with horses and they'd gone horseback riding. He didn't like Shelly going out unless she was with him so during the week she waited for him to leave for work and then she walked down to the Trolley and stayed there all day. She would score there and walk home in the evening and clean up and have dinner waiting for him when he got back. She was a lousy cook and he always told her so. After a time, he stopped wanting to go out, so on Friday and Saturday nights they stayed in. When Shelly asked for money to have an abortion, he said she should use the money he'd been giving her to save for his birthday present, and when she told him she had spent most of that money, he said it was time she left. He put her in the car and drove her back to her mother's apartment and she said, Please turn around, I want to go home, and she cried and told him she'd kill herself if he didn't turn around. But when they were at her mother's complex, he told her to get out, so she got out and waited on the steps for her mother to get off work. Shelly was tired and she could hear the cars rushing up 320th and it occurred to her that it had been nearly a year since she had seen her mother and that maybe she had moved to a different apartment across town or maybe she had quit the teriyaki stand and got a better job or changed cities or moved back home to Korea where she had always said life was better. Maybe she's not here anymore, Shelly thought, and for a second she almost panicked. But that was stupid. She got sick of waiting so she walked five miles to the Trolley and when she got there she was so tired.

III. When he was sure that his wife was asleep, he snuck out of bed and went downstairs and got on his office phone. He called the number and they started talking. She'd been waiting for him to call. She knew he'd call. He wanted to know if she liked to be with men and women at the same time. She loved it. She'd been with lots of women—she loved women *and* men—and she'd been waiting for—No, he didn't like that. OK, she'd *never* been with a woman but she'd always wanted to try. In fact, there was another women with her right now and she really wanted to be with her if it was all right with him. By all means. So she was with another woman, a young coed with long blonde hair, they were both young coeds with long blonde hair, and they were both in their panties—You know what, how about this? She was *with* a young *brunette* coed and *she* was an *older* woman—a friend of his mother's from when he was a teenager—Rebecca White was her name. She had beautiful long red hair. Her husband's name was Dave White and they had two teenage sons. Her husband was obese and she didn't love her husband and what she'd always wanted was *him*. What she'd really always wanted was to be with a bond trader. No, what she'd *really* wanted was to be with a young coed and a teenage boy who might *someday be* a bond trader. The boy has dreams of becoming a professional baseball player, see. The bond-trading thing is a last resort because his dad has a—Some things just don't work out in life. You know what, let's just forget all about this bond-trading business.

OK. They were all together now. The young blonde, that is, the young *brunette* coed, the older woman, that is, herself: Rebecca White, and him: the teenager with aspirations of playing pro ball—You know what, let's just get rid of the coed. It's too confusing with the coed and it's sort of beside the point.

OK. So it was just the two of them. Right. It's just the two of us. The two of us: you, a young baseball-player-in-the-rough, and me, Rebecca White, wife of David White, mother of two, and best friend to your mother. Right. And what am I wearing? She often wore a jogging suit, which I liked quite a bit, but I always imagined she would meet me at the door in a towel and we would proceed to the couch. Are you wearing your baseball uniform? It doesn't matter what *I'm* wearing.

OK, you've just been playing baseball with your friends and you're hot and thirsty and you figure you might stop at my house for a drink of water. I'm all alone. You ring the doorbell and I answer the door in a towel. You can see the tops of my big, round tits. I'm dripping wet. I've been waiting for you. I've wanted you so bad, ever since I first saw you at your mother's birthday party. Do you wanna go into the living room and sit on the couch?

Her breasts were small actually. Regardless—yes, that would be fine.

OK. I take you into the living room. I push you down onto the couch because you've been a bad boy. Naughty boy! I know you've been thinking about me when you're in bed at night, under the covers. I kneel down and unzip you and take your cock out because I've been wanting it *so bad.* Whenever I've been fucking my fat husband. Oh my God, it's *so big!*

I'm sorry; just a second. How about this: I'm remembering a girl in my band class that year. Kimberly Something. What was that girl's last name? Played alto sax. I guess her last name is irrelevant. My thought is this: possibly, she could come out from upstairs. Say she's been up there taking a bath with you or something. I know I nixed the coed thing but maybe it would help if there was another female presence. Tell you what, let's bring the coed back. I'm sitting on the couch and you're in your towel and the coed comes downstairs in a blue and gold cheer-leading outfit. With pom-poms. Shirtless, of course. Wet, soapy breasts. Ponytail. All right?

It's your dime.

Fine, let's do that then. You, Rebecca White, young coed, towel, cheerleading outfit, pom-poms. Me, young pitching pros-pect, sweating hard after a long day of playing baseball with my friends. All right. Let's take it from the top.

Me and my girlfriend Kimberly have been—

You know what, now I'm thinking latex.

Do you realize what this is costing?

IV. Davin and Sarah were very happy and after they married they lived all over the West Coast and spent some time in Texas and Louisiana for kicks. They loved that they didn't need much money and they embraced the punk lifestyle. They spent most of their money on alcohol and records. Sometimes they'd borrow money from friends, and when they had to, they'd each go and apply for a warehouse or a picking job, depending on where they happened to be. They didn't mind the work so much and they prided themselves that they could pick up and move whenever they wanted. If they couldn't afford an apartment and no one was around to let them crash, they'd live in Davin's old Volkswagen bus and shower at the Y. Davin loved Sarah. He loved making her laugh and he really loved the things they'd do in the sack. They would fuck like crazy. There was nothing they wouldn't do together. Sometimes Sarah would dress Davin up in a dress and makeup and she'd put his long hair in pigtails and have him fuck her. Sometimes she would fuck him. He thought she was the greatest and she liked him too.

Davin played bass and Sarah played a little guitar and sang a little although she wasn't the greatest singer. But singing wasn't the most important thing. They would often play with their friends and sometimes record on 4-track. Davin wanted to make it big in the indie scene—he had a dream of being king and queen of the indie scene—and he was good enough to—he was an excellent bass player—and Sarah liked the idea well enough, but she wasn't too optimistic. She thought that Davin would never amount to much of anything and she had always thought this and she told him so whenever she got angry enough. As for herself, Sarah had no idea what would become of her in the end. She wasn't a smart or attractive or talented girl in any way, and she thought, although she didn't want to, that she would go back to South Seattle someday and get a job in a bar like her mother, live in a shitty little house on a piece of dead land like her mother. She didn't see Davin in this picture and didn't mind. She liked Davin, she liked how nice and funny he was, but she couldn't see herself staying with him for very long. In the end, he probably wouldn't stop her from going back to South Seattle and she hated that. He'd want to go with her. What she wanted was someone with a nice job and some money to set her down in one place and make sure she never went back.

Sarah got pregnant in Madera County and when she was almost due, she and Davin drove up to Washington to stay with Sarah's mother in her house. Davin got in an argument with Sarah's mother the first day and she kicked him out, so Davin drove down to his friend Gary's house by the Home Depot in Federal Way. He called Sarah many times a day telling her that they could stay with Gary, that he was going to come pick her up and get a job at a warehouse with Gary and she could stay home all day until she had the baby and afterwards, and Sarah always told him to leave her alone for awhile to think.

Sarah's mother worked all night and slept in during the day, and Sarah lay on the couch all day watching TV. Her mother smoked and drank a lot and looked much older than she was. Her face had deep grooves through it and her nose had been broken before and it was flat in one place. Men would sometimes come over after her mother got off work and Sarah would listen to them fuck in her mother's bedroom, her mother always sounding like the wind was being knocked out of her, and afterwards they would fall asleep and Sarah would hear the man snoring. She had heard these men snoring all her life. After a few weeks, she called Davin and he drove out and picked her up.

They named the baby Dylan after a TV character Sarah liked and when Davin had saved enough money, they moved out of Gary's house and into an apartment behind the Wal-Mart.

Davin worked long hours in the warehouse driving the forklift and he liked coming home to his wife and playing with the baby. They would go for walks with the baby in the stroller and sometimes they'd go on picnics. Davin loved having a family of his own. He'd never gotten along with his family and he was going to do all he could to make sure this one turned out right. He never raised his voice around the baby and he let Sarah make all the decisions. He didn't mind. He and Sarah weren't having sex anymore and it frustrated him and depressed him sometimes, but he told himself that he didn't mind. He always tried to make her laugh. Sarah let him watch porno movies after she went to bed, so he watched them and after he was done he was always very depressed.

Sarah was often depressed, herself, and she didn't like Davin touching her anymore and she didn't know why. Sometimes she couldn't stand the sight of him, and she would stare at him while he slept and feel sick to her stomach. She didn't know why and she felt guilty about it. She loved Dylan and now that she had him, she vowed she would never go back to South Seattle, she would never get a job at a bar like her mother. But she knew that Davin was never going to be able to give enough. She didn't like Davin touching her anymore, but she still liked him and appreciated what he did for her, which was all that he could. One night she came into the living room while Davin was watching a video and she told him to bend over the couch and she fucked him. They felt better for awhile.

Davin kept practicing his bass. He jammed with various people on the weekends and formed various bands that never managed to stay together for more than a few weeks. He and Gary stayed together and they played well together. Gary played the guitar and wasn't bad. He'd been in jail for almost killing a man one night at a bar. The judge had made him take anger management classes. Davin liked Gary because Gary was loyal to his friends and he treated his friends like family and would do anything for them. But one night, when they were both drunk and playing in Gary's basement, Gary got mad at Davin and blindsided him with a shot to the temple. The punch severed the optic nerve in Davin's left eye and left him paralyzed down his left side. When he was unconscious in the ambulance, Davin dreamt he was an old man in a huge mansion with children all around.

Gary was ordered to take more anger management classes and Davin stayed in the hospital and worked on physical therapy. He spent months picking up paper clips and learning how to walk again and he regained some movement and feeling in his left side. Sarah didn't like being at home alone with Dylan and she would bring him to the hospital during visiting hours and they'd stay with Davin and watch TV. Davin was always very happy to see them and he did his best to keep up a pretense of contentment. The government paid the hospital bills and gave Davin a thirty-thousand-dollar settlement that Gary would someday reimburse. Davin's left eye died and turned a very beautiful turquoise color. It shrunk down to half its original size and the doctors removed it. They fitted him with a glass eye. When he went home, he still had trouble walking, and he had no vision in his left eye and only half in his right. He stared straight ahead and walked with his arms dangling loosely at his sides. Sarah thought he walked like the creature from the Black Lagoon.

On the way home from the hospital, Sarah drove the van and they stopped for ice cream and took Dylan to the park to let him play on the jungle gym. Sarah and Davin sat on a bench and Davin watched Dylan, who was now two years old, with his hands on his thighs and his head forward and a sad expression on his face. Sarah watched Davin peer through his periscope. She stared at the side of his face and knew that he couldn't see her. That night they went home and Sarah moved Dylan's crib into the living room and put him to bed and then took Davin into the bedroom and undressed him. She gave him a blowjob and let him come in her mouth, and when he could do it again, she got on top of him, then moved off and got on all fours. After he was done, she lay next to him and looked at the side of his face. He was breathing hard, staring at the ceiling and she knew he couldn't see her.

He wanted to save the rest of the settlement for a rainy day so Davin went back to the warehouse. He couldn't drive the forklift anymore so they had him sticker items. He sat on a chair all day and put the price tags on and sometimes his fingers wouldn't work right, and he was always the slowest one. Still, he kept a good attitude and told jokes and laughed with the people there. Gary had left the state and everyone at the warehouse told Davin that none of them had ever been able to stand Gary and they all wondered how Davin ever had. Everyone liked Davin and he made them all laugh. He started hanging out with a kid named Jim, who hadn't known Davin before the accident, and they'd go down to the Trolley and around to the other bars, and crack each other up, sometimes laughing until they cried. When he'd drink Davin would have even more trouble walking, his left side would seize up and sometimes he'd fall. When he'd fall Jim would pick him up and brush him off and Davin would stand there, quiet, looking straight ahead.

One night Davin came home from the Trolley and he picked Dylan up from the floor and carried him into the bedroom and set him down roughly in the crib. Dylan cried and Sarah ran into the room and started shrieking, yelling at Davin to get away from her son. Davin started crying, himself, out of his right eye, and he kicked the side of the crib and grabbed Sarah by the shoulders and threw her against the wall. She ran at him to hit him but he grabbed her shoulders and threw her against the wall again. He looked crazy. He felt crazy and Sarah was scared. He squeezed hard on her shoulders and pushed her down to the floor. Then he ran out, stumbling as he ran down the steps in front of the apartment.

When he got back early in the morning, he passed out on the couch and woke to someone tapping his shoulder. He opened his eyes and saw a policeman and when he turned his head he saw another one and when he kept turning, he saw Sarah standing in the hallway with Dylan in her arms. Davin spent the rest of the night in jail and he tried to reach Jim to bail him out, but Jim wasn't home and he couldn't think of anyone else to call. So he spent two more nights in jail and when they released him, they told him he couldn't come within five hundred feet of Sarah or Dylan and if he did he would go back to jail for a long time.

He stayed with Jim and worked at the warehouse and saw his parole officer every week and took a drug test twice a month and sometimes randomly. Sometimes his parole officer would take a cup out of his desk and make Davin fill it. They made him take expensive anger management classes and go to Alcoholics Anonymous and to life-restructuring therapy. He didn't have an anger problem or a drug problem or even a drinking problem. He didn't need his life restructured. He was twenty-eight and all that had happened was he'd had a hard year. Half of his paycheck was taken out each month by the State and given to his ex-wife and son. He would have liked to move out and get a place of his own but he couldn't afford it. He'd already hocked two of his basses and his guitar and most of his records and recording equipment, and all the money the State had given him was gone. He missed Dylan and Sarah and loved them both the same as he always had.

After a year, Sarah let Davin come over to the apartment and see Dylan. Dylan had missed his father that year and he recognized him immediately. Sarah sat on the couch and watched Davin play with his son. Davin pulled up Dylan's shirt and blew into his stomach and Dylan laughed hysterically. Sarah liked watching them play together but it made her sad. She didn't know why. She'd been working at a day care for almost a year. At the day care, she'd met a man working construction and they were dating. He lived in South Seattle and sometimes spent the night with her. They were starting to talk about marriage. She watched Davin kissing his son and laughing and she thought about her new boyfriend, the construction worker. He was a good man and very stable. He was what she needed. She was almost thirty and she had a son. She liked the construction worker. He could be mean sometimes and he wasn't very funny but it was all right. He wouldn't let her fuck him but that was all right.

IT'S TAKING SO DAMN LONG TO GET HERE (III)

Somebody passed me a gas mask and I put it on. I tend to get claustrophobic so I wasn't really into wearing shit like that on my face, but I put it on anyway and someone put a joint up to the part where the filter would go—they'd unscrewed it. I think they have better ones nowadays, this one these people got at a junk store. But somebody puts a joint up to that part and I start breathing in. I'm already pretty high by this point, but the gas mask is filling up with smoke, and it's good weed—this was London, so we'd get that Amsterdam Skunk. The guy takes the joint away and I'm supposed to leave the mask on for a minute or so and when I take it off, the thing is, I'm supposed to be the highest I've ever been in my life: *You're gonna fly.*

So I'm sitting there inside the gas mask and for a second I forget about being claustrophobic and not liking closed spaces, I forget all that, I'm just enjoying the high, watching the smoke swirl around with me inside and feeling good, feeling *comfortable*; and then it occurs to me that someone at some point must have worn this gas mask out of necessity. And I swear I heard—you know those people you see in old newsreels, all huddled together down in the Underground and in shelters when the bombing was going on? and the soldiers in the trenches when the bombs were falling, trying to dig down deep, trying to cover up, looking up through the smoke and not knowing where it's coming from, not seeing anything, not knowing when or if or why it's going to come down on them? Well, it was like I was with them, and I heard a voice say:

It is coming down for all of you, everywhere, all the time.

I tore off the mask and ran down the stairs and outside. I stopped in the street, and looked up, then back at the house I had run from. They were gathered at the window, laughing. I looked up and down the road. It was dark and I had no idea where to go.

CHICKEN

We were stopped at a red light on Pac-Highway just past Sports World and this car full of girls pulls up on our left side. This was late on a Saturday night. It was me and Dave and Bill, and Bill says we should race them. So when the light turns I gun it and get a good lead on them, even though my car was a piece of shit, but we're just having fun. It was a guy driving the girls' car, I could see that as soon as we took off, which meant it'd make for a better race, I thought, and he gunned it off the line too and was about to catch up and right when he was almost even, I put some more on it and cut him off so he had to swerve out of his lane and into what had been ours. Bill and Dave were cracking up and telling me to go faster, so I go faster, and I look back and their car picks up speed and the girls are sticking their heads out the window and yelling at us and I thought that was the coolest thing. I cut them off again because a car had turned onto the road in my lane and when they passed that car they got into the lane next to me. We were all laughing and having a good time. Bill kept telling me to gun it faster and Dave, in the backseat, was laughing too. Then the guy put something extra on it, because he comes tearing up to us and goes by—the girls are hanging out the window, flipping us off and yelling, which I thought was cool—then he swerves over in front of us and his brake lights go on. I swerved into the oncoming lanes—there wasn't any actual traffic, so it was completely safe—and we're yelling and I'm gunning it, hoping no cops come and no cars come, and when I'm past him again on the other side of the road, I cut back into his lane, and the stoplight up ahead goes from green to red and I slam on my brakes and skid into the crosswalk, and the car behind me—those girls and that guy— they screech out too, they slide a little and come to a stop about a foot behind me. We were laughing. I looked in my rearview mirror and I could see those girls pointing at us and one in the backseat was standing up and leaning over the seat and talking in that guy's ear, and that guy looked mad, man—he looked really pissed. Then I see him undo his seatbelt and he gets out of his car and I see him walk up towards my car. Here he comes, said Bill and he was laughing too. There were three of us. We could have taken him. I rolled down my window to see what the guy was up to—he was much shorter than me, and pretty stocky—he could have been a boxer or a wrestler, I guess. But he comes up to the window and he's really mad. What the fuck are you doing? he says. What the fucking hell are you doing, you little piece of shit, and I get a twinge of nerves. My heart starts going faster and nobody's laughing in the car anymore. Pull over to the side, the guy says. We'll settle this like men. I don't want to pull over, I say. It's no big deal. It is a *fucking* big deal, he says. Pull the fuck over and we'll settle this like men. The light turned green right then and my foot touched the pedal a little, just a little, not enough to make a revving noise, but a little just to know it was there. I'll take all three of you on, the guy says, and nobody in my car makes a sound, except me and I say, Take it easy, man. I was just messing around. It's a green light, I say, I gotta go, but the guy's got

his hand on the door like he has the intention of keeping this
car right where it is and I feel the gas pedal, but I don't stomp it.
You're a fucking little pussy, the guy says, and his hand moves
off the car and I almost gun it right there—I look up at the
light and at the cars stopped on the corners, and I don't see
his hand—I don't see it—but it does come down and it comes
down hard—he hits me with a straight shot to the face. I put
my hands up to my nose and there was blood. I wondered what
those girls were thinking. Don't fuck with me, he said. Don't
ever fuck with me.

Me and Jim stood in the island in the middle of the big intersection by the mall. Jim was smoking a cigarette and he might
have been stoned. We were there to interview this guy, Mick
Midano, who was running for state senator. We were interview-
ing him for class, not because we wanted to, but because we'd
pulled his name.

"Where do you stand on the issues?" Jim said.

"Put that cigarette out," Mick Midano said. He wasn't looking at us. He was holding a sign that had his name on it, and
waving to people driving by with a big smile on his face. When
he said to put the cigarette out, he spoke out the side of his
mouth.

Jim thought about it for a second, then put the cigarette out.
Later he'd start talking all sorts of shit about it, how he had no
right to tell him to put it out, and I'd bring this all up later in a
conversation with my dad, after Mick Midano was running for
senator of the United States.

"What are your thoughts on gun control?" I said. I was the
one carrying the notebook.

Somebody honked. "Well," he said. "I suppose you'd have to
ask me something a little bit more particular." He never looked

at us, just smiled and waved at cars. I looked at Jim. Jim was getting sort of mad.

"What about abortion?" I said.

"Is this for the school paper?" Mick Midano said.

"It's for class."

"Hey!" he said. "All right!" He was yelling at someone who had yelled something encouraging at him out the window of a car.

"We should push him into the street," Jim said to me.

"What?" the guy said. He was looking at us now. "What did you say?"

We left and drove to Seattle to this passport photo place where everyone was getting fake IDs. I was sixteen and I looked about fourteen, but I got one that said I was twenty-two to make it seem more official. I had to ask the lady what the zip code was for Anchorage and she checked a book for me.

Santos was a basketball star in high school. They went to finals and lost to Bellingham. He scored thirty-six points out of fifty. He walked on at the University but never got a chance to play. This was in the seventies. Anyway, he had a baby with a girl from his high school, Meg, who I met when Santos and I were parking cars in the nineties. I was just out of high school and Santos was getting up there. Meg was picking him up early in the morning after work when I met her. She was a nice lady, although I could tell she probably had other plans once upon a time. Santos was a fast worker, but he always had people yelling at him for moving their seats back. The man was tall. The man still is tall, I guess. We would work graveyard shift sometimes and lie out in the shuttle van. The shuttle van was to take people to the airport or to wherever they wanted to go or to take people from the airport to the hotel or the parking lot. We would lie there and talk about things we liked to eat, or would like to eat if we had the money and the know-how. One night we went to Denny's when we were supposed to be training a new cashier who had come from Ethiopia and didn't speak much English. It was three in the morning and we knew no one would be coming in. We took the van and the radio and we ordered Grand Slam breakfasts. Then something came in on the radio right in the middle of the restaurant. It was Derrick, our boss. Derrick was all right normally, but his wife had just gotten cancer which meant he wouldn't be able to quit his job and go back to school like he wanted. He wanted his wife to support him while he got his medical degree. Now that wasn't happening and he was in a terrible mood. He told us to get our asses back. The new cashier had already screwed up with a customer and had panicked. Derrick found him out back crying his eyes out, and mumbling things in his strange tongue. We jumped in the van and drove back quickly. Santos was driving and swerving at cars to make me laugh and he was smiling because he knew he'd never get fired—and that meant that nothing would happen to me either. Santos was pretty tight with Derrick. Well, it turned out the Ethiopian guy couldn't work anymore. He was a wreck and no matter how much Derrick tried to explain that it was all right, that it was just his first day on the job and things like this happen, etc.—no matter how much Derrick talked to him, the guy only became more confused. Apparently a man had come out of the hotel while Santos and I were at Denny's and had wanted his car to do some late night cruising, and the Ethiopian guy didn't understand him. Plus he was just the cashier. So the guy went into the hotel and talked to the doorman, who said he didn't know where Santos and I were, even though we'd told the Ethiopian guy that we were going to Denny's and to call us on the radio if he needed anything—and the doorman called Derrick at home. Then Derrick came in and called us on the radio and told us to get our asses back. The Ethiopian guy was driving

away all teary-eyed when we got back. I saw him once after
that working at a movie theater downtown. He was tearing
tickets. He seemed to be enjoying himself and he didn't seem
to recognize me, so I just said thank you and walked past.
When Santos and I got back to the hotel, Derrick came storming out of the booth and he pounded on the door for Santos,
who was driving, to open it. He flipped the switch and Derrick
stormed onto the van. The gist was that Santos and me were
fired on the spot and there wasn't any changing things, no
matter what Santos said to try to calm down Derrick, and no
matter how he tried reminding him how long they'd known
each other, and no matter how he tried reminding him that he
had a daughter to support, and that I was still in high school
and saving up for college, myself. Surely he could understand
that, couldn't he? said Santos. But apparently he couldn't. Derrick told us to take off our valet jackets and I did and Santos
said, You're making a mistake, Derrick. Don't make me look
bad in front of the kid, he said, but he took his off too. We
walked home because Santos didn't want to wake up Meg. It
was a long way and we bought 40's and drank them on the road
out of paper bags. I still had a long way to go, but pretty soon
we were at Santos's house and we stopped. I still had a long
way to go. Santos looked at the dark house and said, What a
piece of shit house. He was buzzed and so was I. What a piece of
shit house, he said. Then he told me about the time he was in
the finals against Bellingham, and he'd scored thirty-six points
already, but they were still down by one with five seconds left.
Santos's team had the ball. The crowd was going crazy and Santos's family was in the stands and there was Meg with the rest
of her cheerleader friends all waving their pom-poms. It was
very quiet in his head, Santos said. He didn't hear any of that.
He only heard it later in the locker room, and on the bus on
the way home, and for a long time after that. He said he felt the
aftershocks, but didn't feel the earthquake. They inbounded

the ball to Santos and he took it down the length of the floor, the clock counting down: 5, 4, 3, 2, 1. He told it like this: He gets to the top of the key and he plants both feet and springs up high—he gets the highest and best extension he's ever had, right over the defender, who was seven feet tall and went to some college or other and ended up in the pros on some team or other; Santos lets the shot go and it arcs real pretty—all the pretty girls in the stands and all of Santos's friends are watching, and Meg, too—and the ball comes down, pretty, perfect, right down the middle of the net—swish! The crowd goes crazy. People run out of the stands and hop up and down and some-one breaks his foot trying to jump onto the floor to congratu-late the team. Everyone is throwing their hats into the air, and the team mauls Santos and they collapse into a pile on the floor. For awhile no one notices the refs talking to each other under the basket. But soon they do. The refs talk it over and the crowd turns quiet and everybody's watching the refs now, Santos being the last to see—he's smiling and he's got tears in his eyes and his teammates are peeling off of him one at a time, and they stand there looking at the refs, and Santos gets up and looks at the refs under the basket, too. The refs decide that Santos released the shot after the buzzer, so the basket was no good. Bellingham wins, they said. After he finished telling me this, he tapped his bottle on his forehead and he looked at his house and he hit me on the shoulder and told me I should apply at the place down the street. They pay more anyway.

Sometimes we'd burn past the security guard in front of the school and drive down to the bowling alley where some of us would play pool. I'd play pool too, once in awhile, but I never was very good at it. Sometimes I'd go entire days without making a shot, missing every one.

There were always old men there, old men who didn't have

jobs—they used to hang out at the bowling alley. Unemploy-
ment, I think. One of these men had only one arm and he
used to shoot pool better than anyone I'd ever seen. He'd beat
anyone who came in. His name was Harold. He would beat you
with one arm, and he'd beat you convincingly.

One time I gave him a cigarette and I said, Where'd you
learn to play like that? You mean with one arm? he said. That's
exactly what I meant, but I said, No, I mean, where'd you
learn to play pool so well, Harold? You have to find *something*,
Harold said. You know what I mean? You know what I mean
by that? He took a long drag off of that cigarette and rolled his
empty shoulder around.

A long time later, I was sitting in the basement of the hotel
where I was working and I was suffering. I had a fever and the
shakes and every inch of my body was falling apart. I thought I
was going to shake to pieces. I thought people were out to kill
me. I thought, particularly, that everyone I saw was hideously
ugly and deformed, and that they were sick too. I planned on
killing myself as soon as I felt better. I had a conversation in
my head with someone I hadn't seen in a long time, demon-
strating in words the gist of my sickness. I didn't know where
she was anymore. She could have been anywhere. I wanted to
get on a bus and find her. I missed her.

Prince got a girl pregnant, a girl named Shawna who used to be
in a class of mine when I was in junior high. I'd had a shitty
year that year when nobody knew me, and Shawna was always
very nice. She was my lab partner and she'd often talk about
guys she liked. I had an extreme thing for Shawna. I thought at
one time that I loved her. Prince got her pregnant a few years
later and I hadn't seen Shawna in a long time, but I mentioned I
had always thought she was a nice girl and very cute. We were
playing in an indoor soccer league. We split when the ball went

up. I ran down the right side towards the goal. Prince ran down the left. The ball bounced off the side wall ahead of me and the defender and I touched the ball at the same time. I pushed him down and kicked it ahead of me and ran after it. Prince was on the left side, swinging in. We were flying. I popped it up over the goalie's head—off the post—and Prince ran in and drilled it into the net on the fly. We laughed so hard we had to call a timeout.

After looking for a long time, I bought some pills off this epileptic at the Trolley. I waited, and finally had to take a bunch at the Greyhound station in Tacoma, and then when we stopped up at Snoqualmie, I took some more. I remember I thought I was an iceberg. I had the impression I was an iceberg. This had something to do with the way I was moving; very slowly. I'd move down the aisle to stretch my legs and I'd get the impression I was a cold, slow body of ice. I get like that sometimes, mostly when I'm on opiates.

But the old guy. He gets on in Ellensburg and sits next to me and starts going on about the Communist Conspiracy and the American Way and how this generation is a generation of spoiled, whiny candyasses. "Not you, of course," he said.

"America is not the place that it was!" he said. "It is a dying mirage! All the men who made it great are dead! All our heroes are gone and now there's nobody! What have you people ever had to *survive?*" he said. "What have you ever had to *suffer?*"

This went on for hours. I'd pretend to fall asleep and he would stop talking for awhile, but he would always start up again, and I'd open my eyes, and if I really *was* asleep, I'd open them much slower.

A few miles before we hit Spokane he starts into a story about Guam, or some island in the Pacific he was on during World War II. I mean, the setup is here's where the old guy's going to get down to business. He knows Spokane's coming up and we're all going to disembark and head off in different directions, so he knows he'd better get down to business. Everything has been leading up to this point. It's been coming. It was all going to eventually end up here.

"Bullets whizzing over my head!" he goes. "It was a massacre! We were running into their fire! They were combing the beaches for us! We were being slaughtered! We were being blown to pieces!" He kept going on like that. The whole bus could hear, I imagine, although no one was saying anything. I just kept looking at the seat in front of me while he told the story, or at this girl across the aisle wearing yellow headphones. My eyes were tearing up from the pills—the old guy goes, "I know, son. Don't be ashamed to let it out. It was a terrible time."

"Darkness!" he goes. "They were right up on us! They were shooting the wounded! Miles of them, as far as the eye could see! So what did I do? I dug a hole. I dug a hole and I covered myself with dirt." This part he was whispering, see. He was whispering in a low voice. We passed an exit sign for a McDonald's. An outlet mall. A Holiday Inn. "I dug a hole and covered myself with dirt," he says. "They were combing the beaches for us. They were shooting the wounded. I dug a hole, so what? So what?" Right about now, he grabs my wrist and squeezes down on it with his hot, sweaty hand, and he puts his face against mine, right up on it. "You think I wanted to?" he says. "You think it was comfortable under all that dirt? You think I wanted to? You do what you gotta do. That's not desertion. Running the opposite way is desertion. Digging a hole is not desertion. Digging a hole is not desertion." And so on.

IT'S TAKING SO DAMN LONG TO GET HERE (IV)

I struck up a conversation with one of the older guys, a contractor—I'd seen his truck outside, a huge white beast with his name and face painted on the side. We drank and laughed and got to know each other a little. For some reason I asked him if he'd been in the War, Vietnam, and he said, No, I had a high number. I didn't have to worry about that shit. I stayed here and took care of all the pussy. Somebody had to do it, he said. There was more pussy than a guy knew what to do with. Pussy everywhere. Black pussy, white pussy, yellow pussy, green pussy, and he laughed.

And then a chill hit us and we turned around and another of the older guys was walking in. He shut the door behind him, quietly. He walked with a bad limp. He was squat, and fat, he had a big handlebar mustache and a round, bald head, but long, dark shoulder-length hair coming down from the sides. He worked stocking shelves at the grocery store where I bought my groceries. I talked to him sometimes at the bar, but usually at the grocery store I hid from him, I tried to pretend I didn't see him, because I understood that there was pride involved. One night a few months before all this, at the bar, I was drunk

and lonely and I was asking him a lot of questions. I asked him
if he'd been married and he told me, No, but there'd been a
woman once, a long time ago, and he'd found her in bed with
a friend of his. He'd heard her from the hallway, and he went
towards the sound and opened the door, and there she was, on
her hands and knees in front of the guy, screaming into her
pillow. He said he just stepped back and closed the door, quietly. He wrote her a note asking her to leave and he went to a
movie and when he came back she was gone. I asked him about
his family. His dad had been a rich doctor in town, he said, and
his dad had died of a heart attack one night in the bathtub and
he and his brothers had carried his dad, who was a very
large man, into the bedroom, where they dried him off and
dressed his corpse and put him in bed and pulled the blanket
to his chin and tied a towel to hold his chin and waited for
the priest to come. After his dad died, he lived for awhile with
his mom and his brothers but his mom had developed some
serious mental problems over the years, made worse by the
death of her husband—who she'd loved dearly, he said—and
she began to think that Jesus was on the other end of the telephone, and he would hear a voice from his bed late some nights
and he would get up and follow it into the kitchen and find her
talking in nervous whispers into the receiver, to Jesus, who she
was sure was on the other end. He would tell her, He can't hear
you, Mom, and she was always so sure that He could. And it
went on like this for a long time and when she finally began to
realize that Jesus wasn't on the other end, what was left inside
of her was a deep sense of abandonment, of betrayal, and she
began lashing out violently against her children, and herself.
She used her fists and knives and whatever objects her hands
could turn into weapons. They took her to a hospital on the
Peninsula and her parents, his grandparents, had finished raising him and his brothers—and they were poor people, but they
did what they could—until they died, and by then he and his

brothers were old enough to fend for themselves, so they went their separate ways. One of his brothers stayed in town and went to jail for running over and killing a cop with his car, and the other, one day, just disappeared. That was before the Government called me up to fight, he said, and I asked him about that: What was it like? I'd read books, of course, seen movies like everyone else. Tell me about it, I said, and he turned away from me and lit a cigarette. He said, No, I don't think I'll talk about that, and didn't say another word to me the entire night.

Well the contractor who'd had the high number, he turned towards the door when his back got cold, and he saw this other guy limping up to the bar, right as he was in the middle of telling me about all the pussy he had while everyone else was off fighting, about the black pussy and the white pussy and the yellow pussy and the green pussy, and when he saw the guy limping up, who he knew—who he knew better than he knew me, definitely—who he knew better than I did, surely—who maybe he had known before the War because it had been a much smaller town back then—well he watched the guy limp up to his stool down the bar, and he stopped laughing, he stopped talking about pussy, and he watched the guy climb onto that stool and yell at the bartender about fifty bucks he was owed on some game or another, he watched the guy laugh about it, watched him try to get comfortable on that stool, watched him rub his gimp leg as he laughed and in a joking manner slammed an empty ashtray on the counter and threatened to jump over the bar and beat the shit out of the bartender; the contractor watched all of this quietly and never taking his eyes off the guy, he said to me (or maybe not to me):

I shouldn't have said that. It wasn't the right thing to say. It was a stupid goddamn thing to say. Fuck me, he said. Fuck me.

He got up and went over and sat on the other side of the guy with the bad leg, and slapped him on the back. He bought him a drink.

Is anyone among you suffering?
Let him pray.

JAMES 5:13

VITALITY

SPAREMAN: When it was late, before he took his triazolam and got into bed, before the triazolam eventually put him to sleep, Charlie would go into the bathroom and kneel over the toilet. But nothing ever came out. He couldn't handle the idea of putting a finger down his throat; if he could, he knew he would feel better. It would clean him out. He wouldn't feel so filled-up all the time, he might not be so goddamn fat. Charlie would spit into the toilet and flush and go back to bed, wait to fall asleep.

He was thirty-five now, and an insomniac. And fat. Fat around his legs, his waist, his chest, shoulder blades. He'd never been attractive—not really—but he had never been fat like this. Not that he was obese. Nothing like that. But his body was filling out, he imagined, like a middle-aged stockbroker's body would fill out, like the body of a man with a wife and a house and a family.

Charlie didn't have a family. He had co-workers, acquaintances. He knew a few people around his complex but not their names. He tended bar at the Trolley. Customers would stay until close talking to him.

You ever been in love, Charlie?

Nah.

Not ever?

Nope.

And it seemed true; that he'd never been in love; he couldn't remember a time when he'd felt even a real, true longing for someone. Couldn't remember anything beyond that plain and simple urge. Nothing strong. There were a lot of guys he wanted to fuck—or *would* fuck if the opportunity arose—Hell, when it came down to it, he'd fuck almost anyone. Like most guys. But was there anyone—had there ever *been* anyone—that he had ever really wanted?

When it was late and the pills were taking a long time, he wished he could be back at the Trolley. Because he liked the Trolley: the smoke, jukebox, pull tabs, pool tables. He enjoyed pouring drinks. He enjoyed the regulars, listening to their stories, their talk about their lives.

Well I've been in love, myself. Too many times.

Yeah?

Too goddamn many times.

Charlie had been there six years. He'd come in one afternoon for a drink and the owner had told him a story about his daughter; how she'd had a boyfriend who'd cheated on her with her best friend and how his daughter had given the boy a second chance, how they'd been drinking at a party one night and had left early to get her home by curfew, how the boy was driving fast and missed a turn and ran the car off the road and walked off without a scratch, leaving the girl in the car, and how the girl, the owner's daughter, had died. He offered Charlie a job, at first as spareman, covering shifts when someone couldn't make it in, working when extra help was needed, then after a time Charlie got the early Happy Hour, seven to nine weekday mornings. People would come in on their ways to work, or after long hours on a late shift. Some of them dirty, foul-smelling, tired. Some of them shaking, sweating, in pain. Charlie would pour them tall, stiff ones; listen.

Now he worked the last shift—six to close. He issued you home.

And he was a generous pour. He made sure the bathroom was clean. And when there wasn't any music playing he'd give you money from the till for the jukebox. When someone put a song on he didn't like, he'd come out from behind the bar and kick the side of the machine until the disc skipped. Everyone would laugh. Sometimes you'd put a particular song on just to see him do this. He hated country-western.

Sorry, Chuck. Forgot you didn't like that one.

Yeah...

The bar would laugh together.

He hated the queer bars in the city—the glaring dance music—the heat and the nausea—and a sense of being caged—always too much senseless, flighty noise. They were like overgrown children out there. The flamers, the queens, the razorheads. None of them were real. They were characters like you would read about in a story. He'd fucked from them occasionally, in his younger years—there'd been a short time when he'd felt almost obliged to go to these bars—but he had never been able to talk to them, hated more to listen to them speak:

What's this one's problem? He don't talk?

He never talks. He just comes here and stares at all the ladies.

That right, Superman? You just come and stare at all us girls?

Cat got your tongue?

During the days Charlie would call down to the Trolley and see if they needed extra help, and on the nights he wasn't working, he would go down and sit with the regulars. He'd scope out the place for straight-looking gays like himself. They rarely came in. But when they did, they'd come in pairs. He'd introduce himself, hang out and play pool with them. After a few drinks he'd feel better, he'd be loose, he'd talk close, rubbing a hand across a shoulder when they'd make a good shot or miss an easy one, always smiling and laughing, drinking a lot. He'd show the same attention to both, never wanting to alienate one or the other. His voice would get louder into the night. By close most nights he could barely stand, and he'd walk out with them, telling jokes and laughing and yelling in the parking lot behind the bar, rubbing their backs, squeezing their necks, leaning up against their cars, until they'd say goodnight and help him to his car and open the door for him and sit him down in the seat and reach across his chest with the seatbelt and strap him in, pulling the belt snug, then pat him on the back or squeeze his shoulder or mess up his hair, then leave, and Charlie would sit and watch them get in their cars together, watch their dark outlines talk and laugh, sometimes kiss each other in the dark of their cars, and he would wish to go home with them. When their lights had disappeared up Pac-Highway, he would start his car and drive to his apartment, feeling sick again. He always had a hard time getting to sleep.

Thirty-five now and getting fat.

And he thought about it for a long time and there'd been a time, hadn't there? A time when he was younger and he was consumed by love? It had taken him over, body and soul, like a spirit. When did that part of himself take leave? How could he have lost it? It had been there once, hadn't it? It was there once. He was sure of it. And now:

Will it just keep going on like this? They drive away at the end of the night and you get older and fatter, and sicker, you stay alone? His liver will give out on him in twenty years and then he'll die. But twenty years is a long time to go on. Like this:

When the pills were taking too long, he'd lie awake searching for the good things, but when he'd finally fall asleep, deep into the morning, what would come to him was always the rest.

You look like shit, Charlie. What'd you do last night?

Nothing. The usual.

Yeah? Well you look like shit.

I'm getting older.

Older! He says he's getting *older!* Man, you still got a long ways to go.

He felt better when he'd drink. And he could work better when he was drinking. If he kept it under control, everything was better. He remembered:

A long time ago—when I was seventeen—high school—there was this kid I really liked a lot.

Oh yeah?

In answer to your question of awhile ago.

Right. I remember.

We got along well.

And that was love?

I guess it was.

What happened?

Jesus... Charlie thought about it. I don't know. I guess... I don't remember.

The boss warned him. Drink on your own time. I don't want to cut you loose, but I will. I don't want to but I'll cut you loose.

But he kept it up. He was warned not to drink on the clock—he was warned many times but he kept it up. And he got fired. He'd started early that day. He didn't keep it under control. He pulled a customer's beard—*Looks like a pussy!*—he grabbed another by the collar—*Two fucking years and you never tipped me once!*—he threw ice, poured free drinks—*On the house!*—he kicked the jukebox until the side caved in, he kept kicking it until you saw the machinery. He kissed a boy's mouth, told his girlfriend she better watch out. *I'm coming for him!* he said. Everyone laughed. They saw it was all in good fun.

Get out, his boss said.

What?

Get your shit and leave. Just leave, Charles. His boss walked away and began wiping down the tables.

Charlie went home. He took his pills and undressed. Stood in front of the closet mirror, naked. He squeezed his fat in his hands, pinched all over: his shoulders, his chest, under his arms, his lower back and waist. He rubbed his hand along his belly, he stroked it. But he was so ugly.

He couldn't sleep.

What if he went into the city? Ordered a coffee and sat outside at a table on the sidewalk? Watched and waited? Surely if he waited long enough there would be someone—if he waited long enough there might be someone who—

Charlie longed for him—the pain in his gut—and he was beautiful—and if he couldn't be with him—his heart was going to—and the passion in his face—and he would die—and he held him and kissed him—and he held him close—and ran his mouth—every inch—and he swallowed him—and he filled him—and let me drink from you—let me hold you—and drink from me—let me eat from you—and tell me—taste me—swallow me—swallow you

No.

No.

Because he was sure that first he had to vomit and get all that shit out of him, so he got up from the bed and went into the bathroom, leaned over the toilet and coughed. He could taste it down inside, but nothing would come up. He flushed and, because he didn't want to go to bed yet, he went into the kitchen, pulled the seal off of the dish soap, turned the water on, made sure it was warm enough, but not hot enough to burn

him, left the water running and walked around the apartment
looking for dishes. He found a glass in his bedroom, a spoon
on a table, a plate with dried tomato sauce on the floor by
the TV. He could hear the water running in the kitchen. He
looked around more until he was convinced that he had all the
stray dishes, went back into the kitchen, stacked them with
the other dirty dishes in the sink. For awhile he stood at the
sink letting the water run over his hands, then he washed some
dishes and set them on the rack to dry and was sure he felt it
coming so he ran to the bathroom, knelt down, put his face
over the bowl, coughed and retched [Oh how I want to love
you! Oh how I want to love you! How I want to love you!], but
nothing came out. He rested his forehead against the back edge
of the seat. He said,

   Hello?

He said, *Hello?*

He cried, *Hello?*

DAMAGE: There was one girl in a glass booth and you
saw her when you walked in. She did a private deal that you
had to pay a lot of money for. You paid and then she'd draw
the curtain so no one outside could see in, and you'd go into
a private room and she'd be on the other side behind the glass
and she'd do to herself whatever you wanted. We walked in and
Nate and Lahti and Jim went straight for the quarter booths—a
row of booths where you go in and for a quarter a shade goes
up and there are two or three girls in a mirrored room, dancing and shaking it, and I think a quarter gets you ten or fifteen
seconds. You get the picture. They come up to you and they
put it up to the glass. The other guys went right for them, and
I meandered in the hallway. I saw that the girl in the private
booth was motioning me over. I walked over. Come in, she said.
You could tell that's what she said, although you couldn't hear

her. Maybe you could hear her, but it would have been an unintelligible muffled sound. Yes, I think I definitely heard her. I'm remembering now. And another thing I'm remembering is this feeling I got looking at her. She was wearing a lacy baby blue outfit. Come in. She had brown, frizzy hair. Come on in, she said. And you look at her while she's motioning you in, then you look back at the desk by the front door where the bouncers are—two big fags with hoop earrings—and then you look back at her and her mouth, and it occurs to you that this girl is in a cage. And even though you're fucked up and dried-out and numb and dumb, the significance of this does not escape you, and you suddenly feel sorry for the girl, very sorry for her, tremendously sorry for her, even if she doesn't feel that way for herself, you do. Even though you are not the greatest person in the world. Really fucking sorry, man. Then you just smile at her and walk down the hall and wait outside the quarter booths, and you hear your buddies inside whooping it up, and you check out the pictures on the walls, black and white line drawings of naked women, and you check those out for awhile, and then there's nothing else to do, so you find an open booth and you go in. I only had two quarters so I put them in. There was a redhead girl with huge knockers and a skinny Asian girl off to the side dancing. They were doing this in front of two windows, side by side. They were both wearing only black pumps. They were dancing to music that made you feel like you were being gassed. Which they pumped through cheap speakers into your booth. The skinny Asian girl did twirls and the redhead girl kept putting it up to some guy's window. You could see every side of these girls, thanks to the mirrors. They were pretty far away and since I didn't have any more quarters, I wished one of them would come over to my window, since my time was running out. Then the redhead girl saw me. She took it off that guy's window and danced down the line of windows in my direction. She looked at me through my window and smiled and really started strutting her stuff. I took my eyes off her for a second and I saw my reflection in the wall of mirrors facing me. You don't exactly see your reflection. You see a dark shape with various light spots that you recognize as your face. Then you try not to look at that because it looks ugly, and you look back to the redhead girl and at her huge knockers and her bellybutton ring, and it occurs to you that whatever is going on, whatever the situation, whatever is going on in her life or in the world, or in your sorry fucking life, in your sorry, pathetic melancholy existence, whatever—this girl is beautiful. Beautiful. And then almost at the exact second that she puts it up to the window, the shade goes down and you're out of quarters. But that's not even the point of the story. When I came out of the quarter booths, Nate and Lahti and Jim were standing in front of the girl in the private booth, looking at her through the window, and Nate was smiling and sticking his tongue out at her, and putting his tongue up to the glass. The bouncers were coming out from behind the desk right as I was coming around the corner, so I was behind them. One of them started pushing Nate and calling him shit, telling him to get the fuck away from that girl or he'd call the cops, and Jim smiles all crazy, and thinks for a second and then he pulls back and crosses the first bouncer up. It gets pretty wild and the first bouncer ducks down while Jim pounds on his head and the second bouncer reaches down and comes up with a billy club and Lahti clocks him one under the jaw. I can hear the girl in the booth screaming now, and she's pounding on the glass, and then—because what else is there to do?—I jump in and start wailing on the backs of their heads. I really pound the fuck out of them. I pound the Living Holy Fuck out of them. Wait a minute. Wait a minute.

ACHE: It began when

It began when he dove into the shallow end of a pool and hit his head on the bottom. It was before his senior year in high school and the world had been turning for a long time and he hadn't been happy in a long time, and when he came to the surface, he felt an ache. He climbed out of the pool and when he could stand, he dried off, went into the changing room, put on his clothes, and drove himself to the hospital where they X-rayed him and said that everything was all right. He had been lucky. He could have broken his spine, been paralyzed, gone brain dead. He could have died. They told him he had a concussion, but the effects of the concussion would pass. His neck would be sore for awhile and he would be confused and his head would hurt, but these things would pass.

The headache didn't go away. He had trouble remembering things and often became lost in conversation. He would know what to say, but not how to say it. He couldn't say it. He couldn't sit still. He couldn't keep his head up. He could not look you in the eye. He found himself afraid of noise.

At school he had a hard time sitting in one place and sometimes he'd find himself rocking back and forth, sweating, and he would have to leave. He tried to ignore the pain as well as he could, but it was useless. Sometimes, he could function. Sometimes, he couldn't. When he couldn't, he'd get in his car, drive through the trees, down the winding roads by

There were more doctors than anyone could keep track of; there was the family doctor and then there were physical therapists, chiropractors, neurologists, an osteopath, acupuncturists; all of whom had different ideas as to the cause of the problem—they all agreed that it had all begun when he dove into the pool, but MRIs and C/T scans showed nothing, and they all had different ideas as to why the problem had stayed so long. They also had different ideas as to the solution to the problem, and according to their specialties, they gave him drugs, and herbs, and exercise regimens. They stuck him with needles and cracked his joints and attached electric probes to his head and neck and shocked his nerves. They made him drink tea made of bark and roots. His family doctor, the doctor who cared the most, gave him pills and made him keep track of his progress in a journal. The doctor made him rate his pain each day on a scale of one to ten and it drove him fucking crazy. He hated to pay attention. And the headache never stopped for a moment.

Once every couple months or so, he would become aware that he was breaking down under the pain. For a week the pain would

For a week the pain would become increasingly intolerable and then finally, it would show itself in all its glory. When his body broke down, when the pain became glorious, his mind would break down and complete things. His mind would give in to the pain and the pain would take control. He would hyperventilate. He would cry. He would have no idea who or where he was.

The first time was six months after the accident. He was lying on the couch watching TV and he noticed that he was breathing in short seething breaths and that he'd been breathing this way for a long time. He could understand what they were saying on the TV but he didn't know why it was such a big deal. He didn't know why they were all wearing blue T-shirts and standing in such a large kitchen. He didn't know why they were all wearing blue T-shirts and standing in such a large kitchen and he slid off the couch and began crawling on all fours. He crawled around the basement like this, crying and shrieking and attempting to hide beneath a desk, then coming out and trying to hide beneath the couch. His mother found him and panicked and cried herself and touched him, pleading with him to tell her what was wrong. What is it, honey? What's wrong? Tell me what's wrong! He didn't know but he was sure that he was going to die. He tried to hide beneath her skirt.

When this happened, and when it would happen in the future, his mother or father, and often both, would drive him to the emergency room where they would explain to the people there his situation, and the nurse would come in and give him a very large dose of Demerol. His parents would make sure the dose was a large one. His mother would cry. The Demerol could not release him from the pain completely, and this always depressed him later. But it took the pain and put it somewhere else, pushed the pain outside of his body, gave him what he needed to breathe right again. The Demerol would give his mind and body a few hours to collect themselves, to restore themselves,

to restore themselves, get themselves into a position where they could once again ease and ignore a small but important portion of the pain, enable him to live with it, as tentatively as he did, which was the best that he could hope for. And it fucked him up and he loved being fucked up.

Among the drugs his family doctor prescribed were a number of antidepressants. His doctor thought that since nothing showed up on any scans, and since he (the doctor) had never seen a case like this in twenty years, quite possibly a large part of the problem, maybe the problem, itself, lay in the psyche. The doctor thought his patient might be depressed and because of his depression, was remembering a pain that had actually long since disappeared, that the symptoms, while they felt real and true, that the symptoms, while they felt real and true, were nothing more than memories. The doctor sent him to see a psychiatrist, a woman with a small office and long, wavy hair. She was attractive, which didn't mean anything, and when he sat down across from her, he felt like throwing up. He hadn't wanted to come. He didn't need a psychiatrist. He wasn't going to tell her any

There was the possibility that he was being punished for something he had done a long time ago. Sometimes, when no one was home, he would lie on the floor, seeking God, first repenting, then asking Him where He was—why wasn't He here?—telling Him there was no way he could go on—Where the fuck are you!—and screaming at Him—What the fuck are you doing to me you sick fuck? Aren't you my father? He broke a window in his parents' bathroom and cut his arms with it. He would take his pocketknife and cut deep gashes in his arms. He would drive the winding roads by the Sound and want desperately to swerve into a tree. He would aim and when he felt the dirt under his tires, he would swerve back onto the asphalt. Aren't I your son? Headache.

He didn't tell the psychiatrist about these things, or anyone else. There was something wrong with him, he knew that, but it wasn't depression. It wasn't depression and it wasn't guilt—it wasn't memory and it wasn't simple but it *was* simple, it was pain and pain was simple and real and true and beautiful and unrelenting and vital as a sixth sense. He loved it. The psychiatrist told him to:

Go down the pathway...through the tall grass...visualize a blue sky...feel at peace...go into the control room...look around... look for the switch...the switch says **PAIN**...I want you to turn the switch off...turn your pain off...turn it off...walk outside again...

He never went back to the psychiatrist. The acupuncturists and osteopath thought they could help him and wanted to see him more regularly, but his insurance didn't cover them, and he felt guilty about having his parents foot the bill for something that wasn't working. The pain didn't leave him, he still had trouble sitting still, he still became lost in conversation—he would know what to say, but not how to say it. After high school he moved out and got a job and took classes at the University, and quit. He dated girls here and there and sometimes got them in bed. He loved lying with them, touching them, smelling them. He tried to live a normal life, was sure that he was never going to be well again. He drank a lot and when he'd drink, he would feel somewhat better. The alcohol would numb the pain to a certain extent, make him forget for awhile, but afterward

His family doctor kept prescribing drugs and the doctor would consult the latest health and pharmaceutical magazines and prescribe the latest drugs and he would feel so tired, his mouth was dry all the time, he couldn't shit right. Every two months or so, he'd have a breakdown and end up in the emergency room. Afterward, he would sit on the steps outside his apartment smoking a cigarette, enjoying the recuperative process, and lean over, slowly, gradually, until his cheek was against the cement, watch the cars slide in the warm rain, he would breathe slowly.

This is how the next few years passed for him—and there were many other things I could mention, things that would take me too long—and he was very hopeless, because he had learned over these few years he had learned that when you're lost in the well, when you're lost in the well and you continue to hope, with each disappointment the bottom drops lower until the world outside the well is only a speck you have to squint your eyes to see. But still

he lived. He moved around and had different shitty jobs here and there. He went out and got drunk and smoked weed—he laughed with his friends, told jokes. Every few months it would happen again and if someone was around they'd take him down to the emergency room and for a short while he wouldn't have to squint to see you.

It occurred to him to get away. So he saved and sold his car and went to London. He got a job and did too many drugs and drank too much, and never slept and worked too many hours, all with the vigor of a man attempting to kill himself. He was in much pain and he met a girl there who wanted to marry him and he overdosed one night and she kept him awake and he clawed at her face one night and hit her and she took him to the emergency room and in the taxi on the way he laughed hysterically and screamed and moaned and couldn't stop laughing and the English doctor gave him a shot of morphine and some Valiums and Vicodins to last the next few days and when they arrived at the flat it was morning, his girlfriend went to work, he took all the pills he had, he smoked some hash, he walked to the Off-License, came back, drank until she came back and screamed at him.

He decided to go back home to Federal Way because he was thirty pounds underweight and dying, and he said goodbye to the girl at the train station and she cried and gave him her guitar and told him to learn to play it, she said she would join him later when her visa came through and they would live together and he would play songs for her. He didn't want her to come and he never saw her again. He was seated over the engine of the plane and for eleven hours he held his head in his hands. He looked down and saw the Atlantic Ocean. He saw icebergs melting on the Hudson Bay. He looked down and saw Canadian tundra. He saw Seattle and he saw Federal Way. He looked for the street he grew up on but couldn't find it and this was a disappointment and after he landed, his father took him to see the family doctor and he cried and held his head and the doctor gave him an unlimited prescription of a strong narcotic—a real ass-kicker—unlimited either by accident or because there was nothing more the doctor could do and he was tired and sad, himself, about the way things had turned out.

He got an apartment and a job. He met girls here and there who wanted to relieve him of his pain and he lived with some of them and they'd pick up his drugs from the pharmacy and stop by the liquor store before coming home and they'd rub his neck and they wished they could relieve him of his pain but they couldn't and eventually he'd meet a woman he would love more than anything in the world and he'd leave for a short time and come back again and marry her.

But for now, he bought furniture and a car and stayed high and drunk for a long time. He lost more weight and popped pills all day, lost jobs and found new ones, tried to live his life in this manner until it became necessary that he quit.

He held his pain and kissed it and stroked it, he told it he loved it more than anything, he loved its vitality, and begged it to leave.

And many years later, when it went away, many years later he would find
he would find that he missed it.

EVERYONE IN THE WORLD: The trick, he said, is to refuse to believe that any of this makes sense. Because when it does—when the world and life and the way things are make sense—then you know there's really something wrong with you.

You get me? he said.

This world should be incomprehensible to us.

Rape shouldn't make sense and murder shouldn't make sense and neither should car wrecks and bombings and loneliness and cancer and diabetes and television.

But usually they don't bother me that much, he said. I usually don't think about them. All I usually think about is: I feel good. Or: I feel bad.

But when I'm feeling really bad and I can't score and I start to get the pain, it generally turns into something more like: the world is sick and everyone in the world is sick, and I'll see some random person and I'll know that he's a child molester, or that she's some diseased fuckbag, except it's much worse than that—the way it feels and the things I think about them are much more awful than what I just said.

And the scary thing is, when you're in that condition, when you get the pain, it all makes complete sense. Of course everyone is sick! Of course everyone is deranged! Because *you're* sick and you're convinced you're seeing them for what they really are.

But really, he said, you don't know them from Adam and they don't know you and I don't know you and you don't know me. Jesus, I don't know myself half the time.

And you shake and sweat and can't sleep and your body aches and you can't breathe and you want to die.

And you know this isn't the way you're supposed to feel and you know you're not feeling things the way they really are, but this time you're wrong.

The pain of living, he said.

Because we hurt all the time, without knowing it. Our bodies ache all the time and we don't know it, because we got endorphins constantly shooting off inside us, blocking all that out.

Without endorphins, we'd all be junkies.

A girl told me this once, he said.

And when you're on opiates for a long time, your body stops making endorphins and when you try to kick or when you can't score and you get the pain, what you're feeling is the way it really feels to be alive.

And it's a terrible thing, he said.

That doesn't make sense, I know, I know. None of this makes any sense.

But if I scored, he said, and I'm feeling good, then it's: *It is well, It is well.* Everything's good. *I'm* good. I don't have to think or worry about anything. There's no pain anymore for anyone anywhere.

It's: I'll just float around in here, nice and toasty, for awhile.

MODERN COLOR NO. 20: Sammie found a baggy of pills in the couch. Probably thirty or so. They had *W-E-L* pressed into them. What the hell was *W-E-L?* She didn't know. These weren't hers and she'd never seen Nate with them. They could have been there for years. She couldn't remember the last time she'd cleaned the couch. She was excited. She hoped they were painkillers (she had an ulcer and when she'd burped that morning, about a teaspoon of brown liquid had come up and she'd spit and washed her mouth with mouthwash and had felt so tired but now) she hoped they were painkillers, but they could always be something worthless.

So she looked in the phone book and called Poison Control. A woman answered.

I need help, Sammie said. I found a bag of little red pills in my son's bedroom. And I don't know what they are.

He's not on any medication?

No, he's not on anything. They say *W-E-L* on them. They're very small.

It's best not to jump to any conclusions, the woman said.

Oh, I know.

They could be anything. Or nothing. He could have just found them somewhere, himself.

Yes, I know. He's a good kid.

They're all good kids. Be careful not to rush to judgement, the woman said. I have a son, myself.

Do you? Sammie said.

He's seventeen. There's a lot of pressure these days.

There sure is.

It's not like when we were kids, the woman said. We had pressures, but it wasn't like today.

It's a different world.

How old is your son? the woman asked.

Fifteen, Sammie said.

Does he keep active?

Sammie thought about it. He's pretty active, she said.

Into sports?

Yes. And your son?

My son, the woman said. He was on the swim team at school. He's been swimming since he was five. He wanted to be an Olympian. He quit awhile ago. Without telling us. He just quit.

Well, maybe swimming isn't his thing, Sammie said.

He's an excellent swimmer. He could have got a scholarship. Maybe gone to the Olympics.

Well, it might not be too late. Maybe he'll want to get back into it later.

We hope so. He put on a lot of weight. I think he didn't like people seeing him in his Speedo. Plus, I just don't know about these friends of his.

Now about these pills...

Oh, I'm sorry. Really, I wouldn't be surprised if they weren't anything.

So you don't know what they are? They say W-E-L.

A pharmacist would be able to tell you better than me. Just don't panic about it. There's probably a simple explanation.

Yes.

There's no manual for being a mother. It'd be nice if there were.

It'd be nice.

You just learn as you go along, don't you?

Yes.

Look, the woman said. I know it's none of my business, but it's important you don't jump to any conclusions. You could end up pushing him away.

Yes. I know.

Our relationships are fragile.

Yes.

Then you'll wish you could take it all back.

I'll keep that in mind.

Yes, I hope so.

And good luck with your son, Sammie said.

They grow up fast, don't they?

They sure do.

They grow up fast and leave us behind. Sometimes it's like they don't like us anymore.

Yes, Sammie said. I know.

You just hope they turn out all right.

You hope.

You only want what's best for them.

You do the best you can.

You can't do more than that, the woman said, can you?

THEY ALL WAIT FOR YOU (SO LONG, PART I): Dying didn't really matter to Dan. It was just another one of life's great kicks in the nuts. He didn't give a shit about it one way or the other. What he hated was sentimentality; he hated the TV shows where the man lies in his bed and his sons and his wife come in and they all forgive each other, and cry, and the man dies, but he dies with peace. Those shows could suck Dan's dick. There was no point in turning—just because a guy was on his way out.

There was cancer in him and he had waited too long. Now he was going to die. He felt fine—he was in OK shape—he didn't feel that bad now and it really didn't matter. One thing was for sure; he wasn't going to let himself get run down—he was not going to go like that. He would take himself out when he needed to. He would not waste away. Life wasn't that important. He'd been in 'Nam for Christsake. He'd learned a thing or two about life. When he went in they called him Baby-san, and when he came out, twenty-three months later, they called him

Papa-san. He knew something about death. He knew it could be long and ugly and painful and specific, or it could be short.

After the diagnosis, he went down to the Trolley. The doctor had tried to put his hand on Dan's shoulder, to comfort him. I really don't give a shit, doc. Really, it's no sweat. I really don't give a shit. Just leave me alone please. Then he had gotten lost walking through the hospital, forgetting which door he had come in. He could not remember the door. He found himself in the cafeteria and decided to sit down and eat. He was feeling tired and weak. He sat for a long time, without rising to get food. When someone sat down at his table, he got up and tried to find his way out again.

No one was at the Trolley but the bartender and a fat woman on the solitaire machine. Dan had been coming to the Trolley for years and he rarely talked to anyone. Hardly a soul. The bartender's name was Charlie and Charlie knew Dan's name, or once had, but neither had ever really called the other by name. Dan spurned company at the bar and everyone knew it. He didn't want to know everyone's business. He didn't want everyone knowing his. It was none of their goddamn business. The last thing he needed

Where was he going to go after the Trolley? Where he was going to go, he had no idea. He stayed on his stool and kept drinking while the bar filled up; people came and sat on each side of him, drank and talked. Dan kept his head low, his shoulders high and squared, he drank, looked up at the TV. He hated TV. But look at those young girls and their young bodies... Jesus Christ. There were some things he would miss.

Probably should give the ex a call. Probably should talk to his son. Dan wondered where his son was now. What was he doing? Out of school, into a job. Married, maybe. Kids? Grandkids? What's next? Death? Dan wasn't going to work anymore. He was going to stay in bed and read history books. He would read history books and watch baseball during the days and come down to the Trolley in the afternoons and drink. He had enough money saved up to live like this for awhile. Enough to last six months, anyway.

It was no big deal but it was just so goddamn confusing. He just didn't get it. He'd always kept in pretty good shape. He didn't do drugs. He didn't smoke. Occasionally he'd get loaded, but who didn't? He had escaped the war without major injury. He had not gone down the path so many weaker men had gone down upon returning. He had lived through a car accident that should have killed him. He slept eight hours a night. His mother was still alive at eighty. Dan wasn't even sixty. He should call his mother. She was the one he should call first. She'd cry for him. He could see her dropping the phone and sobbing into her hands. She would be hysterical with grief. Well... It doesn't matter much now anyway.

Yes, when the time came he would do it himself. No use dragging things along. Getting sloppy, lying around a hospital ward, puking all over yourself, waiting for your lungs or your heart or your brain to give up on you. No use lying around in pain, staring up at the fucking TV, unable to walk or talk or piss or shit by yourself. He'd seen it happen to his old man. His old man had gone like that. His old man, he had gone that way.

But goddamn, wasn't this a piece of bad luck. You just never saw it coming, did you? You just never knew it was coming for you.

Someone would have to take care of his dog. He didn't want them sending that dog to the pound after he was gone. He'd have to make arrangements. It was a good dog and he loved it. He loved it and he would miss it. Maybe he wouldn't have the chance to miss it. He hoped he could miss it. He'd rather not—He'd rather not just close his eyes and *that's it*. He hoped there would be something more. An afterlife. Supposed to go somewhere. Someone to welcome us. Goddamnit, where the fuck was his refill? Can't you see I'm empty?

After the bartender filled his glass, Dan threw another dollar on the counter and went into the bathroom to piss. He pulled his dick out and shot into the trough.

It was going to hurt. There was going to be a lot of pain. He'd been in enough pain during his life and he knew that what was coming would be much worse, much more insistent. He didn't want to live the rest of his life in pain and he didn't want to live like a junky. He'd like to get laid again. He'd like to go back to Vietnam. He'd like to see his wife and his son and his mother.

Some punk was sitting in his seat when Dan came back from the bathroom. Whaddya mean you didn't know someone was sitting here? What the hell is that fucking beer doing there, Einstein? Don't tell me to chill out, you little pissant! Don't you talk to me like that! And then the bartender came over to settle things down. I've been coming here for fifteen years, Charlie! I don't want some punk kid talking to me like that! I was coming here when there were woods across the street! You wanna tell this little punk to—

I hear you, the bartender said. Relax. Your next one's on me.

Jesus Christ, there were some things he wouldn't miss!

Where was

And where is

Fuck it. Fuck God. Fuck Jesus. Fuck Allah. Fuck Mohammed. Fuck Buddha. Fuck it. Fuck all of them.

They'd never been around when he had needed them. There wasn't any use hoping now. Maybe he would say a prayer right at the end and settle things. But that could wait. Maybe he wouldn't say a prayer, after all. Fuck it, they were never around. Who cares?*

So what did he have? Man, I have nothing. He wanted to go home and see his dog, but he didn't want to get off the barstool quite yet. He wouldn't call the shop and tell them anything. He just wouldn't show up anymore. He'd let them wonder—he wouldn't answer the phone and then after awhile they'd get the message—send someone around to his house—he'd tell them, I quit, I'm tired—they'd move someone up to foreman—maybe Keith—they'd probably give Keith the job—Keith would make a good foreman. Maybe after awhile he'd call Keith and wish him good luck.

Dan drank a few more, watching the TV shows—those motherfuckers wouldn't know drama if it bit them on the ass— and then he got up off his stool and nodded goodbye to the bartender. The bartender nodded back and said, See you tomorrow, and Dan nodded his head again. He put his jacket on and headed towards the door. Then he thought about it and—Wait— turned around, slid his jacket off his back. Maybe I'll have another one. Give me one more. No point in

* I.e., maybe there is no Savior and no one is coming and no one will ever come.

INTRODUCING...

You didn't know what to say to something like that. But I wasn't surprised. I'd known him since we were kids. I just moved on to the next thing. He was living then in Sea-Tac and wanted to get together sometime—he wanted to start a band—and when it was his stop, he rang the bell and stood up. He gave me his number at what I assumed was his sugardaddy's house and I told him I'd give him a call which I never did. We'd used to do a lot of drugs together and now I had different people I did drugs with. So I didn't call him. But I did always wonder what happened to him.

Well, I'm cleaned up now and much better, and I've got a little girl. It's true that you start thinking about the world a whole lot differently when you have a kid—I mean, the world seems a lot more dangerous now that she's in it, when back then it was all kicks. The world didn't seem so diseased, so sick. There didn't seem to be anything particularly wrong with it, and with the way we were living, but now that she's here, I look back and think about some things and it really gets me down sometimes. It's hard to explain.

But I was walking into the mall the other day and somebody yells at me out the passenger window of a truck, and I stop and the truck stops, and Brent gets out. I hadn't seen him since that time years before on the bus. He looked a lot better—he was bigger, he looked like he used to look, the way I remembered him from growing up—a little older, maybe—a little fatter—he still—he would always get these little white bubbles around the corners of his mouth when he talked—I'd always assumed they were from using—he still had those and he wore a pair of dark sunglasses. I asked him how he was doing and he said he thought people were following him all the time. He said he thought he was famous and everyone he saw, he thought he should recognize them, and he should recognize them because they recognized him and that was because he was famous. He told me this very matter-of-factly—he wasn't freaking out or anything, just making observations. But he said that, although he knew in reality it wasn't true, he couldn't shake the feeling that there was a conspiracy going on, that everyone he saw was looking at him, that he had become famous, but for what he didn't know.

Sometimes, he said, I could just about kill somebody.

There were certain things that I still felt bad about, ways in which I had dealt with him poorly in the past—things I should have done differently, treated him better and so on—I wanted to know what else was going on with him, how he was doing, and he told me he was living with his dad, that he was off everything—no speed, no downers, no acid, not even weed anymore. He'd been on Zoloft but he wasn't taking it anymore because it gave him a headache. He said his head was much clearer now anyway but he was tired of thinking that he should recognize everyone, tired of thinking he was famous, tired of wondering why he was famous, tired of thinking about how tiring it is being famous, because he knew—and he stressed this part— *that he was not famous in the least*. He was working graveyard shift at the Circle K and he'd just gotten off and he liked the job because it was quiet and he could think better late at night and in the early morning because everything wasn't so chaotic then and there weren't so many people around, and this town is too full these days, he said, there are too many people, too many stoplights, too many banks, clothes and grocery stores, too many fast-food restaurants and bargain warehouses, too many people he doesn't know, more people than he has the capacity to know, who don't know him and don't have the capacity to know him, too many traffic jams these days, and there are Circle Ks all over the place and it's very easy to get transferred to a different one and, someday, move to a different town, out of Federal Way, which is what he wanted to do. I said, Didn't Circle K merge with British Petroleum? because I wanted to show him that I was interested in his life and he said he didn't know, BUT THERE ARE EIGHTY-THREE THOUSAND EIGHT HUNDRED FIFTY OF US AND WE'RE NOT EVEN ON THE MAP.

His dad was waiting in the truck, so he had to go—I don't really know what else we talked about—something else—I remember he mentioned he had run into an old friend of ours recently and that the old friend had told Brent that he and I hung out once in awhile. I hadn't seen that guy in a long time, either. I'd wondered about him also, and I couldn't figure out when I had hung out with him last. In fact, I knew I hadn't seen him in years. When did you run into him? I said, and Brent thought about it and said, About two years ago. Then he gave me his number and said we should get together. It had been nice to see him—it put a lot of questions to rest, but I didn't really want to see him again. I told him I'd call him. I said it was good to see him again and I hit him on the shoulder.

ONE MORE

The dead man took a deep breath and walked inside—OK—and—Get it together—to the back. He handed the phony prescription to the girl behind the counter and she looked at him, said just a moment, then went into the back room. He tried to keep cool. Turned and looked at other customers, smiled, looked up at a security camera, smiled nervously. He shifted his weight as if to ease a pain. He tried—bit down on his lip—to think—he took a quick wet breath through his nose—tried to control his breathing—tried to think of and focus on—to breathe right—something that would steady him.

The pharmacist cleared her throat and dialed 911. She had remembered his face. Nicely dressed. He was black but that didn't matter; what mattered was that he was back. She hoped he wouldn't get scared and leave. The woman on the line told her to stall him until the police arrived. If he wants to leave, don't attempt to keep him there, but stall him if you can. She said they'd be there soon.

The pharmacist took a moment to steady herself. Looked in the mirror. Her heart was beating fast. Fixed her hair. OK,

Relax. She took a drink of water from the cooler, wiped her lips, a deep breath, and walked back out. She told the man it would be another moment, someone was filling his prescription in the back. She made small talk so that he wouldn't leave.

What did they talk about? Later, when people would ask, and later, while she was alone, she wouldn't be able to recall.

That they talked about the elections, and of the consequences of the current drought. They talked about the weather, and the cold, and about how dark it was so early now. He'd been on the boats up into Alaska, and he'd seen the weeks and the months when the sun wouldn't rise at all. It stayed hidden just below the horizon for so long, and of course there were the Northern Lights, and

as he shook, as he shook and drew quick breaths, and as his eyes watered and he cleared his throat and cracked his joints, as he told her about the waves of light,

at that moment, though she wouldn't remember it, the pharmacist was remembering a painting that had been hanging in her family's garage when she was a child, a painting of a yellow sun rising into a vivid orange sky. She had loved that painting and now she wondered where it had come from. Who had painted it, and where had it gone? Had her father taken it with him when he left? Had her mother, perhaps seeing something in it that she hadn't, thrown it away?

The pharmacist nodded and stepped back and looked to the floor. Let's go. The cops took the man out, past the makeup aisle and checkout lanes and people standing in lines; they led him out, one on each side. Sat him in the back of the squad car. Now sit tight.

No need for handcuffs, no need to pat him down.

He was old and tired and well-dressed.

They went back inside and interviewed the pharmacist. They asked her questions and took notes. This sort of thing happened all the time and they weren't in any hurry to take the man in. One of the cops wanted to take the pharmacist home and make her. She was sexy as hell. The other was remembering something significant that had happened to him as a child, something that had only recently resurfaced during therapy, something he hoped no one else in the world would ever know. None of it was your fault she said. She said none of it had anything to do with you.

The pharmacist answered all their questions with the utmost gravity. But inside she was very excited, slightly tremulous; she looked forward to telling her roommate all about it when she got home. Her heart beating fast, she opened a bottle of spring water and took a sip, could see through the window, the red blue lights raced around the telephone pole across the street. Shadows seemed to cross themselves, then back again. Nothing like this had ever happened before. And she had handled herself well.

When she heard the shot, the girl dropped her bottle and crumpled to the floor and the cops, stumbling as they drew their guns, ran to the door *[electrically, hypothalamus sends a message activating adrenal glands, muscles tense as heart rate and breathing increase, capillaries close, blood pressure soars, eyes dilate, digestion stops, as does sexual functioning]*, swung around and saw the man, dead. Rear window red, clots of blue and gray matter—the matter—clinging to falling from the glass. The two of them stood, clutching their heads. What was the meaning of this strange Vision?

A group of shoppers realized that they were not alone. They looked at each other, confused, looking for answers. Then walked to the door, and stood inside, looking out. At the three men battered by the lights. Beyond them, the night was dark and cold. Cars drove by. The pharmacist stood and brushed herself off, her memory already retreating into the night. Everyone agreed they'd all thought they were going to die.

GUNMAN

The man who boarded the 96 Shoreline–Downtown Express, waited awhile, then shot the driver in the chest, and then himself in the ear, causing the bus to career over the side of the Aurora Bridge fifty feet straight down, killing one passenger and wounding the thirty-two others onboard, wasn't the same man who swiped the motorcyclist on the interstate, exited his car and jumped the sound-proofing wall, ran erratically through a neighborhood and bludgeoned an old woman watering her lawn, only to be killed within the hour by a bullet to the head from a SWAT sharpshooter's rifle.

Earlier this man (the second) had murdered his mother and eighteen-month-

old nephew in their suburban tract
house with a kitchen knife. He was
twenty-one years old, a good basketball player, enrolled in junior college,
a friend to many in the neighborhood.
No one had seen it coming.

And no one now has any explanation
for what he did. He'd had minor
brushes with the law before, but nothing serious—certainly nothing that
would have led one to expect what
was to come. He was a little odd,
they say. A little odd, but really nothing more than that. He was friendly,
kind. He loved his mother dearly. The
gunman's father, who won't speak
publicly about the incident, has told
friends that the gunman was deeply
devoted to her. There are reports that
he loved, also, his young nephew. No
one knows what was going through
his mind.

What we do know is that around three
o'clock PM he entered his nephew's
downstairs bedroom and stabbed him
repeatedly in the chest. He then
attacked and killed his mother in a
similar fashion in an upstairs hallway.
A neighbor reports seeing him pull
out of the driveway and drive out of
the cul-de-sac at a high rate of speed.
He did appear to be troubled. Tears

were running down his cheeks and his lips were moving as if he were talking to himself in great agitation. We know that from there he drove onto the freeway, headed north toward Seattle, and, at speeds of eighty miles an hour and more, swerved at passing cars, clearing a space for himself three lanes wide.

The people in their cars, many of them driving home early from work, pulled over to the side and let him pass, with the exception of a sixty-four-year-old man riding a Honda Gold Wing touring bike in the slow lane, who refused to pull over and was clipped from behind by the gunman's 1993 Toyota Celica.

The motorcyclist spilled over, trapping his left leg beneath his bike, and slid thirty yards down the pavement before coming to a stop. His leg was shattered, in places the bone scraped down to the marrow. Doctors at Harborview Medical Center removed the leg later that night. He reports feeling much better today, but still suffers pain where his limb used to be.

Possibly foreseeing that the police would now be involved, the gunman pulled to a stop. Witnesses report he signaled before pulling over, sat in the car, his lips moving furiously, pulling at his hair at times, staring blankly into his hands at others, before finally bursting from the car and scaling the concrete wall that had been put up decades before in an attempt to sound-proof the new neighborhood from the onslaught of ever-increasing traffic noise.

On the other side of the wall, parallel to the freeway and branching from a dead-end street, was a dirt driveway that led to a small shed beside a house with an upstairs view of the freeway. Beyond the shed was a ravine, shel-tered by trees, a small creek running down its deep and narrow center. The gunman chose to go left, toward the street, and into a neighborhood, away from the shed, away from the ravine, which he may not have known was there. According to people who watched from their windows, once on the street, the gunman ran up the north sidewalk, eastward, a metal object (later reported to be a pipe he'd picked up from the side of the free-way) flailing wildly at his side, his limbs, they said, loose and helter-skel-ter, a puppet on strings. His face was wide, his teeth showed clenched. His eyes, they noted, were full of fear.

An elderly woman, two blocks east of where the dead-end street met the freeway wall, was watering her lawn, hose in hand, shooting a stream of water up into the air from a metal attachment. As the gunman approached her, running in that same erratic manner, he shouted. The woman, still holding on to the hose, became afraid and attempted to run in the opposite direction. According to witnesses, even had she chosen another direction—*any* other direction—there would have been no chance for escape. The woman, moving very slowly in her old age, stumbled over the hose and fell to the ground. She frantically called out to her next-door neighbor, a twenty-eight-year-old man sunning himself in his backyard. The young man got up from his blanket and looked over the fence. As the old woman attempted to lift herself to her feet, the gunman, wielding the metal pipe, began battering her about the head. Witnesses say the old woman lost consciousness and remained motionless as the gunman continued to beat her. She died.

The young man shouted out to the gunman: "What are you doing here?" But he reports that there was nothing he could do.

By now the police had been called
onto the scene. Officers at the gunman's suburban home were finding
the bodies of his mother and nephew;
officers and an ambulance crew were
now attending the fallen motorcyclist. Probably hearing the sirens,
the gunman ran another block and
attempted to enter a large two-story
tan house on the north side of the
street. The front door was locked, so he
went around to the back, scaled a pylon
and entered through an unlocked door
on the upstairs deck. It's not known
exactly what his next course of action
was, but one would surmise he then
went from room to room, searching
for weaponry. We know that he did
this at some point, because eventually
he found an unlocked gun cabinet in
the master bedroom belonging to the
head of the family, a thirty-seven-year-
old machinist, husband and father of
two high-school-age girls.

The unlocked gun cabinet contained
various types of hunting rifles, a
.45-caliber semi-automatic handgun,
two World War I vintage rifles, a
20-gauge single shot shotgun, two
semi-automatic machine pistols, and
over 100 rounds of ammunition. Hanging from a hook was a black kung fu
robe with a red dragon insignia.

The gunman removed his clothes and put on the kung fu robe.

Now armed, he must have walked down the upstairs hallway, past the lady of the house's collection of ceramic Scottie dogs, down the stairs, and into the living room, facing the street. He closed the curtains all but a crack and backed the couch up against the front wall, below the windows. Then, he waited.

There are a hundred things the gunman might have done in the moments before the police arrived. From autopsy reports we know that he did not eat, he did not defecate, he did not consume drugs or alcohol, he did not masturbate, nor vomit. He probably watched television, which was found turned to the news after his death. He probably talked to himself, nervously. He probably pulled at his hair at times, and stared blankly into his hands at others. But what else he did in those last moments before the police arrived and the shootout occurred, we can only surmise. It is up to the reader to speculate for him/herself.

Soon, news and police helicopters were flying high above the area. Police

were barricading the street, evacuat-
ing residents through their back doors.
SWAT teams were called in, placed
on rooftops throughout the neighborhood—a multi-tiered net was con-
structed around the house. The freeway was closed in both directions. A
nearby elementary school was locked
down, the classrooms locked, window
blinds shut.

From aerial shots taken above the
scene we see men in black crouching
on rooftops, squad cars in formation,
blocking exits and entrances, officers
crouched behind their cars, arms outstretched, guns in hand. We see the
brown-shingled roof of the house
where inside the gunman sits; the
back deck, patio furniture, a scorched
lawn. But nothing happens. Some
report seeing the curtains move from
time to time in the living room, but
the gunman only sits and waits. What
he is waiting for, we don't know.

Nor will we ever know what pos-
sessed the thirty-nine-year-old U-Dis-
trict man to shoot the driver of the 96
Shoreline–Downtown Express, then
himself, causing the bus to plummet
fifty feet off the Aurora Bridge, only
yards before the point where the bridge
begins its stretch over Lake Union.

An East Coast native, trained as
an architect, the gunman had been
retired for years due to a troublesome
back. He was not supported by the
government, he received no Unem-
ployment, L&I, Workers' Compensa-
tion—besides social security and bank
account numbers, the government
had no records of him at all. Instead,
he received a monthly check from
his parents, a well-to-do couple in
their eighties residing in a suburb of
Newark, New Jersey. The mother of
the gunman reported later that he
had been a normal child, a normal
man, that he had never been known
to have significant psychological problems. He was a kind and gentle person,
according to his mother. Two weeks
before the incident he had paid a visit
to her New Jersey home. There had
been no warning signs, she said, other
than a certain irascibility.

The gunman, called by Seattle Metro
officials "an habitual bus user", was
a man obsessed with schedules. After
the incident, police would find current
bus schedules taped to the walls of
his meager basement apartment. They
would find stacks of outdated schedules, many from other cities. Alumi-
num foil had been stapled over the
windows, blocking the light from out-

side. Garbage spilled from garbage
cans. Food was rotting in the refrigerator. The police would report an over-
whelming filthiness, an overwhelm-
ing squalor.

Taped to the walls, below the bus
schedules, were notes detailing the
busses the gunman would ride, and
the dates, fares, and times of each
ride. He would tour the city on busses
at all hours, planning his destina-
tions beforehand, most often having
no reason to travel. He was known
to complain loudly if a bus were late,
or if conditions on the bus were too
warm or too cold. He would pace the
aisle, opening and closing windows.
His mother has stated that he'd often
phone her long-distance, complaining
when a bus had not arrived on time.
On the wall beneath his notes were
charts of alternate bus routes, with
times, pick-up and drop-off points,
should any of the busses he'd been
trying to take not arrive.

After the incident on the Aurora
Bridge, the gunman was identified as
the man who a month earlier had
jumped onboard the 72 University–
Lake City off-peak and put a gun to the
driver's head, pulling the trigger twice.
The gun made two sharp clicks. The

gunman jumped from the bus and fled.

When police responded to the scene below the Aurora Bridge they found people wandering around bleeding and disoriented, they found men and women lying on the ground with lacerated kidneys, lungs, livers; they found a massive wrecked articulated bus lying on its side, people trapped inside, piled one on top of the other, some crammed in the small spaces beneath their seats. They found the body of the gunman and that of the driver, holes in each of them, eyes closed, chest to chest.

One passenger died later of internal wounds at Harborview.

Another had an arm and a leg removed. Today he lives with government assistance in a housing project in the Central District.

Most of the witnesses hadn't seen what led up to the accident. Most don't remember the gunman getting on the bus. The ones who remember hadn't thought anything of him at the time. He was dressed in dark slacks and a white, buttoned dress shirt. He was clean-shaven. His hair was dark

and cut short. He was not the sort
of person you would have worried
about, witnesses say. You would not
have looked twice. But the ones who
remember say he boarded the bus two
stops before the place of the shooting
and sat down near the front in a side-
ways-facing seat. He held on to the
rail and stared out the front window.

What was going through the gunman's
mind at that moment, we don't know.
How did he choose his moment? Why
hadn't he used bullets in the attack
on the 72 a month earlier?

There are pictures of a mangled metal
bus, rods and wires, opened and torn
from the inside like the corpse of a rotting animal. Firemen cut through the
wreckage to free passengers. There
are close-ups of hands and faces. On
our TV sets, we see the lights of the
ambulances rushing over everything.
People stand around watching, crying.
The victims huddle under blankets.
That's how we know who they are.

Why do these things happen? What
is it that allows them to happen? We
wonder if there is a higher order to
the universe. We wonder if there is
a higher order to our world, at least.
We report that our world is falling

apart. And we report that we are falling apart.

As the bus approached the bridge,
the gunman stood, reached into his
pocket and pulled out his gun, then
walked to the front, where he shot
the driver three times in the chest.
Before turning the gun on himself,
the gunman took hold of the wheel
and veered the bus off the bridge.

The bus shattered the concrete railing and plummeted fifty feet into
the garden of a Fremont apartment complex.

IT'S TAKING SO DAMN LONG
TO GET HERE (V)

Then there was nothing. A dial tone. I'd hung up on her. The first time I called back it went to her voice mail. So I hung up. Then I called right back and it started ringing but then nothing—I thought she answered it but just wasn't going to say anything—you know, the silent treatment. I said, I can hear you. I know you're there. But I couldn't and I didn't. Finally it went on too long so I figured there was a problem, and I hung up and called back. I got her voice mail again. I left a message: Baby, I'm sorry I hung up. I'm trying to get through. I hung up. I called back. This time it stopped ringing and she answered but here's the thing: it was *her* but she was this tiny little voice, this still quiet voice that sounded so far away. You could have breathed over her. She said, hello? hello? Then she paused. hello? And I'm talking back at her the entire time: Baby? Can you hear me? But she just said hello again and hung up. I called back. It went to voice mail. I hung up. Called back. It happened again. I mean, she answered it. hello? And now I'm nervous. This tiny little voice calling out to me through space, an *enormous* space, and I'm nervous and I'm praying she knows I'm there, I'm getting desperate, I'm yelling into the phone: *Can you hear me? Can you hear me? Hold on! I'm trying! I'm sorry I hung up! I'm trying to get through! I don't know what's happening! I'm*—But just ...hello? And then she hung up.

IT'S TAKING SO DAMN LONG
TO GET HERE (VI)

I'm walking out the door and I turn around and I wave bye for some reason, and I don't even know who I'm waving to, I don't know *now*, and I probably didn't know *then*, and one thing I notice as I'm walking away is the lawn could really use some watering because all that's left is practically dirt, and when I walk down the walk, dust and dirt go swirling up in the air around where the grass should be, which is another weird thing, because also it gets really windy, then it stops, then it gets windy again. But anyways the grass needs watering so I make a mental note to water it later since there's no time, and it's not my house anyway, it just appears very obvious that it needs to be done. This is all occurring to me in seconds I think and by the way I'm carrying a briefcase and wearing a suit which is odd for me, I'm sure you'll agree, and I'm smiling although I don't know if I can see the smile, or feel it, because really, this one was so strange I can't remember if I saw everything from inside my skull, like with my own eyes, or if I was following myself, like panning the scene with a camera and I'm just watching it. I'd have to say if I thought about it, this part I was probably seeing it like it was through a camera, but from here on in I'm back in my head again, and I stay that way until the end, I know that because what happens becomes very personal to me, like I'm not just watching it on TV—what happens isn't special effects, although like I said, that's how it was in the beginning because I do remember seeing the suit, and me in the suit, and thinking how dumb it looked on me. So I walk out of the yard and I guess I'm just walking down the road or something but the next thing I know I'm getting on a bus and the bus driver looks at me and says, "It's on me," or something like that, and I'm relieved because I don't know if I have any change because these aren't my pants or something, I don't know. A lot of this is pretty murky. But we get going in the bus, and I don't know where I'm going, or like why I'm wearing this suit, and these kids on the bus, these punk rockers, these kids like the ones I used to hang out with before that big problem I told you about, they start going, Look at the suit, and, Check out the suit on the man, and shit like that, nothing really mean, though, not the way I used to be, nothing violent or obscene, just sort of observations, and maybe a little bit of respect—I don't know, it's all just a bunch of weird shit. Then one of the kids goes, *Jesus!* and he's looking out the window and there is a bright orange sky like you have never seen, like you could have painted orange all across it, like the orangest color in the world, that's what the sky looked like, and I'm talking about the entire sky, no matter what window you looked through the sky was bright orange, and behind us it was too, and through the windshield it was orange. And then what happens is the wind starts going again outside the bus, the trees start really moving and things fly through the air, and then I see we're coming to an airport and the driver drives onto the runway and stops, and it's like becoming obvious to me the way everyone's turned around in their seats and staring, that this is my stop. So I make my move and I walk down the aisle, and this redheaded girl with enormous boobs goes, like, BLESSED ARE THE DEAD WHO DIE IN THE LORD FROM NOW ON, and she squeezes my hand, and I go, What? What's that supposed to mean? What are you talking about? and it starts getting really trippy because everyone stands up in their seats and starts clapping, like they're applauding for me, really applauding and I'm sort of thinking they're all crazy or something, but I do a sort of little bow and step off the bus, and when I'm off the bus, they drive away, and I'm convinced those motherfuckers are the craziest motherfuckers in the world, and I look up at the sky again, and I can't really tell you much about it except it was very orange and if the sky ever turns that color, you will know that something big is about to go down. I remember standing there looking at all that and the bus driving away and thinking, I wonder what that chick meant about Blessed are the dead who die in the Lord from now on, like what could she possibly have meant by that, and I start walking onto the runway, because it's suddenly obvious, I don't know why, that I'm supposed to, no matter what might go down, and there aren't any planes or anything—the whole place is deserted. No cars, no planes, no people, nothing. I just keep walking until I come to the middle of the runway, far away from all the buildings and everything, just asphalt and dying grass, and I walk the line—you know the line they paint in the middle—I walk that line for awhile and this is a long runway and I'm not getting anywhere so after a few minutes I get the feeling like I should sit down. And now comes the part that is the hardest part for me to explain, because what happened was I sat down in the middle of the runway and I started crying. I'm not talking about just cry-ing either, I mean, this wasn't normal, there wasn't anything normal about this; my eyes are going crazy and I'm rolling around and I'm whimpering and I'm sobbing, like anybody would take one look and go, that motherfucker has got a lot on his mind. And afterwards, like even now, I've been trying to put together why I cried like that, when it's not in my nature, and I came up with that it's not subconscious or anything, and it doesn't have to do with growing up, even though I had it rough, or with how hard or disappointing life seems to be; anyways, the point is, I wasn't crying for myself, but for the world. I don't know how I know this, but I do. I've been putting it together and this is what I've come up with. When I was crying I felt like the entire world was wrapped around my back and it knew it was dying and it had this heaviness to it like you probably get when they're about to pull the plug on you and you're laying there thinking, *I didn't know when I started that it was going to end up this way.* I don't know how long that went on for but at some point I stopped crying and I think it was because I heard a noise, like a roar—I know I heard the noise, I just don't know if that's what woke me up—*something* did—and the next couple of minutes are a little blurry because what I am doing in the next couple of minutes is waiting for the roar to get closer so I can make it out, because now there is a dark spot against the orange sky, and it's getting closer and I'm waiting, and I don't know what I was thinking while I waited other than it's taking so damn long to get here, and I'm tired and I feel like I've been waiting all my life.

FISHBOY

Shortly before I turned eighteen, my dad drove me across the country to begin a college career in fisheries at a less than half-rate school in Nebraska; fisheries being a field that at the time I believed to be the source of all true knowledge. No matter what the true source was, or is, I wasn't having any luck getting into four-year schools, and, not too long before graduation, I received a letter in the mail offering me the opportunity to enroll. I didn't remember applying, actually. In fact, I don't think I did. But things had not been going well for me at all, and when this school said that they wanted me to come and, yes, they did offer classes in fisheries, I thought that someone in this world of sorrow had finally been born with good sense and that I'd better go.

I hadn't seen the old man for a long time before our drive because there'd been a night when the girl he'd been sleeping with had shown up on our front porch with a suitcase in her hand and nowhere to go. There was a big and very loud row, during which my mother—a woman who honestly hadn't been in her right mind for a long time—was, in spirit at least, wounded mortally. She was doped up on a mixture of Valium and alcohol and this probably should have served to deflect the brunt of the wound, but when she answered the door and that girl started talking, I think something inside of her broke, whatever that string is that holds a person together, it snapped. She came to life for a second and screamed her head off—she made a very high-pitched shrieking sound that I could hear from my younger brother's room—and then she stopped; she stopped yelling, then stopped talking, and wouldn't start again. My dad left us that night and disappeared for a long time and my mother upped her intake, spending all her time in front of the television or shuffling around the house, holding on to pieces of furniture or my brother's head to keep herself steady. It was heartbreaking, really.

This wasn't the only reason I was troubled that year, or the reason I ended up where I did, but it did tend to complicate things. There were other significant components. For one thing, I had developed an obsessive preoccupation with a girl at school two years younger than me named Emily Swanson. Also significant, I was suffering from an irrational but very real fear of paralysis that had developed over the course of my adolescence. I was afraid I might cross the street one day and something crippling would happen—a car would come barreling around the corner, say, and send me into orbit. Maybe something would fall on me—a block of ice from the wing of a plane—and shatter my spine. Or I'd be forced into a situation where it would be the heroic thing to do to throw myself in front of a runaway train to save a girl, always a particular girl, from harm. And when, in my imagination, the train would break from the tracks, headed, at a speed of more than a hundred miles an hour, straight for that particular girl, who was usually sitting in a patch of grass with her legs tucked neatly beneath her, reading or dozing under the afternoon sun—when, with the roar of crunching metal and battered earth, the train would be almost upon her and she'd look up from her book or open her eyes from her nap—when the shadow would fall across her face and I, close by, would ponder: Should I throw myself in harm's way for her?—when in my imagination I would hold off the train, stopping it for a moment in its tracks to give me more time to decide (and I could only hold it off for so long)—Could I save her? Should I save her?—when this situation would unfold in my mind, the girl on the grass was, ten times out of ten, Emily Swanson.

My dad and I drove straight through and arrived on a Monday. There wasn't much to the town. Just a few stores down the main strip, a bank, a movie theater showing two films that had come and gone from my town months before, a grocery store, a car wash, a gleaming Masonic Temple, various statues and monuments. No one was around. There was a ghost-town feel to the place that unsettled me. My dad smiled and pointed. What he wouldn't give to be able to live in a rustic place like this one. This is how life used to be, Will. You don't see this anymore.

We found my apartment a few blocks away. I'd taken it sight unseen—the basement of a run down pre-Industrial era house. We walked through piles of leaves, down the stairs at the side and into what was going to be, from here on in, my new home. I took one look and my heart flipped around and sank quietly into my stomach.

"What do you think?" my dad said.

It was essentially one large room with a kitchen against one wall to the right as you walked in, a thin strip of windows facing the kitchen, and a couch and an alcove with a bed to the left. The paint on the walls was peeling and dingy, the tile floor had dips and little holes in it, the low ceiling was made worse by a network of forehead-level pipes, and the kitchen reminded me—down to the huge metal sinks—of the old moldy kitchens where I would wash dishes with the ladies at sixth-grade camp.

To put it bluntly, we were standing in the middle of a piece of crap shithole.

"It's crap," I said. "It's a piece of crap shithole." And then I ducked my way into the bathroom, locked the door behind me, and stayed there, staring at the red painted floor while my dad unloaded the car.

And my dad, who was a good guy really—a good guy who had become fed up with his family, with his life, and had decided to make a break for it—spent the next five days fixing up the place. He cleaned and painted the walls and doors. He bought me blankets, tablecloths to cover what scant furniture there was, matching towels and dish sets, rugs to cover the floor, fans to combat the heat, a new bed; he filled the refrigerator with food, redid the wiring, bought three stand-up lamps, and handed me two hundred bucks to start a bank account. He set up my fishtank, an old thirty-gallon number I'd found in our garage the previous year, on a small coffee table that he bought at a department store and to make it feel more like home, he used heavy-duty hooks and wires to position a mirror above my bed at an angle so that I could lie on my back and watch the reflection of the tank, close my eyes and fall asleep without moving a muscle. All this he did during the days, whistling away happily while I read comic books or watched my portable television or wrote down my thoughts in the small hand-sized notepad I carried around. And at night, after taking me out to an enormous dinner, he would insist I take the bed and he would take a blanket and a pillow, lie down on a rug next to the kitchen table and go to sleep, bad back, frozen arm and all.

After five days, when he was finally convinced that he had done all he could and I was as happy with the place as I was going to be, he packed up his things into his duffel bag and sat down next to me on the bed. He put his hand on my shoulder and I knew he was about to get at something.

"I'm sorry, Will," he said. "I'm sorry about what happened.

It wasn't fair on you boys. It's just—goddamn it," he said. "I'm really lonely, Will." And then he started to cry.

I sat and watched in amazement until, after about a minute, he blew his nose into his handkerchief, wiped his eyes and said, in a weary and dejected tone, "Your mother's not well, Will. She's not."

This struck me as a departure. "She's all right," I said.

"No," he said. "She's not. I'm sorry but she's not. She needs help."

"She's fine," I said. "You're the one who's not fine, Dad."

The truth was my mother was far from fine and hadn't been fine for a long time. She had tried, when I was younger, to understand the circumstances of what she had felt had always been wrong with her but could never quite put her finger on. She read books. She bought tapes. She sought professionals and listened to them. They took her back to the source. That is to say, she came to understand herself perfectly, and over the next few years she began to sink deeper into pills and alcohol as a means of coping with that understanding. By the time I left for Nebraska, she'd very nearly lost her mind.

"You're the one who needs help, Dad," I said. And then I told him some things I would regret. I told him I didn't care about anything, not about him, not about my mother, not what he did to my apartment or where he slept or how many girls he fucked. I said I didn't care that he had disappeared for so long. I didn't care that he hadn't called, or visited, or checked on us. I said I was glad I hadn't had to see his face. I told him that I really didn't give a crap about any of it and I'd had a shitty time driving to Nebraska with him and I wished he'd disappear again and leave me alone, let me get the hell on with my life. I could tell it hurt him tremendously. He told me he was very sorry I felt that way and then he picked up his bag and left.

When I heard his car drive away, I walked outside, up the stairs and onto the front lawn. It was evening and the sun was gone and the stars were beginning to show up for the night. The sky was dark blue behind me, and lighter, tinged with pink in front of me and I watched his taillights get smaller as he drove back down that road, back toward Washington and his apartment by the airport. I watched those lights for as long as I could, but then they went down something and disappeared. I poked at the enormous cold sore that had attached itself to my mouth as we'd driven into town. I cleared my throat a few times. I spit a big loogy onto the grass and walked back downstairs.

I picked up my notepad and wrote: *The O.M. started bawling. Drove away back home. Good riddance.* I lay on my bed and stared up at my fishtank. My angelfish hovered off to one side staring out of the glass, making gasping motions with her mouth, and my four remaining goldfish swam awkwardly on the other side. Occasionally one would hover over the ceramic castle, or float near the bottom, skin's width away from the rocks. This made me feel terrible for some reason. I went into the bathroom and put some Neosporin and a Band-Aid on the corner of my mouth. I took the Band-Aid off and put it over the whole length of my mouth and looked at myself in the mirror. Then I lay down on my bed again and closed my eyes.

I'd always had an overactive imagination, but during the time I'm talking about this trait became something like a proof to me that I was on the way to losing my mind. It was an issue that concerned me more and more. It was obvious, the way my parents lived their lives, that insanity ran in the family and I, at that point, had done some questionable things myself. But as I was lying on my bed with the Band-Aid over my mouth, I heard something very real, something that had nothing to do with imagination. First leaves crackling. Then slow and heavy footsteps from the stairway outside my door. I turned my ear. My fish turned toward the door. The footsteps—whoever was making them—clopped their way down and stopped at the bottom. For a few moments nothing happened. I could hear myself breathing, the fishtank bubbling. We waited for what might happen next.

The door exploded. A white light filled the room, then a yellow light, then a red light, and a sonic boom, followed by a series of high-pitched screeching sounds. From the opening in the doorway, a long red flame burst in and split the room in half. A tall man walked in. Dressed in a black bodysuit and a gold fireman's mask. He held a shiny gold flamethrower. He walked around my apartment and, slowly, methodically, began to light everything on fire. He opened the refrigerator and stepped back. He pulled the trigger and with a roar the inside went up in flames. He walked into the bathroom, there was a whooshing sound, I saw a glow. Then he came back in, walked across the carpet, and stood in front of me. He spoke words, deep and thunderous but unintelligible behind the fireman's mask. Then he turned back to the rest of the apartment and fired again. The drapes went up and the walls and then the floor, and the fire raged to the ceiling.

I was terrified—I was trembling with fear. When I made up my mind to move—and what I was going to do, I have no idea—flee, most probably—I'm sure if I could have I would have dashed through the flames, ducked beneath the burning doorframe and run off into the fields—when I made up my mind to move, I couldn't. It was as if someone had tied me to the bed, or given my entire body a case of lockjaw. I could only stare up at the mirror. I watched, petrified, as the man in black walked over to my fishtank and sprayed it with flame— whoosh!—the water boiled and my fish burst their seams. The water turned red. I closed my eyes. He came over to the bed and opened them. Shook an angry finger at me. I closed my eyes again, and when I opened them a few seconds later, his monstrous back was passing slowly through the doorway. The flames trailed him like the train of a robe.

The light on the other side of the door went out. The room became very quiet, slightly chilly—no trace of what had just happened, no fire, no smoke, only me on my bed staring up at my fishtank, scratching at my cold sore through the Band-Aid.

But Emily Swanson.

I had, by the time I left for Nebraska, whacked off for a significant part of the year exclusively to the one picture I had of her, which was on a flyer for Ivan's Fish Bar, a reasonably priced fish joint across from the mall, where she worked as a waitress. The flyer had come in the mail one afternoon before my dad left us. I had never seen Emily in the flesh—I had no idea she existed beyond that flyer—and I was struck by the photograph and took it into my room. I think I probably have it buried in a box somewhere. She's wearing a white blouse and showing two rows of perfectly straight, white teeth. Her blonde hair is up on top of her head, a few strands dangling in front of her face. There is a dark space beneath her jawline that may have been the result of a smudge on the camera lens, but I was never able to tell conclusively. *Welcome to Ivan's,* the caption says. *How can I help you?* I kept it beneath my bed and took it out whenever it felt necessary.

It probably goes without saying that I wasn't a very popular kid. I'd had a difficult time making connections with people my age, but not from lack of trying. I liked people, or at least, the *idea* of people. At different times in my high school career I'd been involved with choir, band, weight training club, dance club, math club, Young Republicans, Young Democrats, Students Against Exploitation, Students for Kind Relations with Russia, the American Morality Preservation Society, drama club, and more that I can't remember. I spent a lot of time in meetings, and formed the Decatur High School Fisheries Council my senior year, of which I was the only member.

And then my dad broke our hearts and left, and I spent a long time unable to see the good in anything. The world became a place filled with blatant sorrow. I stopped attending meetings. I spent a lot of time in my room with my fish, or in my brother's room, watching him play, or on the couch, watching television with my mother. But one day toward the end of that final school year I was walking down the hall after science class when I saw the girl from the Fish Bar flyer leaning against the wall, her backpack slung over her left shoulder, waiting to go into history. I recognized her immediately and my heart leapt into my throat. I mean it. I had to keep my mouth closed tight to keep from spitting it up onto the carpet.

I bribed a kid who worked in the office to tell me what her name was, what her story was—she'd been kicked out of St Mary's for questionable behavior—what classes she had, what hall her locker was in. I changed my normal routes through campus. I made sure to pass by her locker as often as I could. I spied on her in her classes through the thin strip of window built into the doors and she always seemed bored. I found that she lived just a few blocks away from me on a cul-de-sac that, in twelve years of living in the same house, I'd never been down. And after a few days of careful observation, I discovered that she walked home from school.

On a Tuesday, I managed to catch her at a Don't Walk sign and I offered her a ride home. She looked around and got in. I said hello, and offered her my hand, which she shook. Her hand was very small. I told her a few rudimentary things about my life, true and otherwise, and soon we were outside of her house where, as well as I was able to, I asked her out on a date which she—and I've never understood why—accepted.

I skipped school the next day and drove into Seattle to find a suitable restaurant. I toured eight in the downtown area and finally reserved a table next to a window at a pricey seafood place overlooking the Sound. I washed my mother's car and had it detailed to the bone. I went into what had been my dad's closet and took out one of the suits he had left behind. I had it pressed. I took a pair of his shoes, a size too large, and had them shined. And then that evening I took a shower and washed with fancy soap, combed my hair straight back with gel. I put on the suit and crammed wadded-up toilet paper in the back of each shoe. I made my brother and my mother dinner, fixed her a drink, and on my way out, I straightened the pillow beneath her head and turned the volume up on the television. "Wish me luck!" I said, and I was off.

Emily walked out before I could get to the door. She was wearing jeans and a gray sweatshirt, her hair held back in a ponytail. She stopped in the driveway, looking concerned.

"I thought we were going roller-skating," she said.

I was a bit overcome, and because of this, I couldn't do anything but stare.

"Will?" she said.

"I figured we might go into the city for dinner."

"I said I go roller-skating on Thursdays," she said. "Are you wearing a suit?"

"What?" I said.

"I told you we were going to meet some people," she said. "Why are you wearing that suit?"

"I already made reservations," I said. "I'll be out fifty bucks if we don't show up."

She made a face, squinting her eyes a little in what was probably confusion. "I guess I should go change," she said, and she turned around and walked back towards the front door. "I really wish you didn't do that."

"Sounds like a plan," I said.

We drove to the restaurant, a few miles an hour under the limit and in the slow lane for safety purposes, and everything went extraordinarily well. We ate and talked about school and the world. I told her my dad was a somewhat godlike patent attorney—whatever that was—and my mother was a freelance marine biologist. I created a world for myself that was more hopeful than the one currently developing. I told her I was considering Harvard and Yale, but that I hadn't made up my mind yet. They both seemed somewhat stuffy, I added, and I might decide to forego a year and stay in town. While I was talking, I pictured the two of us falling madly in love with each other and raising a litter of happy little kids. They'd have my blue eyes and her pink complexion and absolutely no resemblance to my parents. We'd be well postured and dynamic and throw dinner parties for the more stable of the families in the neighborhood. But in this fantasy, and in similar ones I would later construct in my head, there were always two people—*figures*, anyway—waiting patiently in the dark on the back patio for the right moment to open the door and change everything. I tried to put them, whoever they were, far into the depths of my mind.

Eventually, because there was no way around it, I had to take her home. She thanked me and I burst from the car and walked her up the driveway, and when we were at the door she turned around and—possibly feeling obliged to—patted my shoulder softly with her hand. And then I made a grab for her breast and tried to plant one on her neck, an act that served to fundamentally change our relationship forever.

I went home and slammed the front door loudly. I trudged upstairs and wrote in my notepad, *Dinner—exquisite. Grabbed Emily's tit. Blew it. We dig our own holes*, I wrote, and attributed the quote to *Anonymous*. I don't think I knew what it meant. I thought she might eventually come around and want to go out again, but she never did. I thought I could convince her to like me again, but I never did. That night I lay on my bed for a long time staring up at my fishtank, and then I drove around looking for my old man's car.

I was coming up with a grand philosophy that I normally believed wholeheartedly, and on my best days, at least half-heartedly. It was that *We live in a world built on sorrow*. That was the gist of it—it's written that way in my notebook—and I'm not sure exactly how I clarified it, even internally, but I think the whole thing had a lot to do with the way my mother had been deteriorating the past few years. It made sense to me that she had tapped into something sorrowful and dangerous about the world and wasn't finding her way out of it. I was convinced that I was slowly tapping into it, myself. The world was built on sorrow, that seemed clear. But I didn't know why.

When Emily wouldn't talk to me, I resorted to strange manifestations of my sorrow. I began calling her at odd hours and asking her questions about sorrow and ache. I'd ask her if one could be sure of anything, really, in the world. Sometimes I would call and not say anything.

She had my number blocked and I started slipping poems into her locker, poems filled with the most obvious and clichéd love imagery, rhymes with words like *parlance* and *substance*, and at the end (after what could be ten or twelve hand-size notebook pages), the last stanzas would inevitably grow darker, the flower would die, the bird would mysteriously fall from the sky or get sucked into a jet's engine; the beautiful fish would flop around without oxygen and die in the throes of melancholy.

A few times I showed up at Ivan's Fish Bar and ordered nothing but water. I'd say that I wished to be served by the young blonde gal from the flyer. She would come out and pour my water silently, without looking at me. The third time I did this, I directed some loud and obnoxious comments toward the rest of the restaurant and was banned for life.

I spent a lot of time sitting with my mother watching television or lying in my room, and whenever I would feel something out of the ordinary, something I was sure was a creation of my own mind, a breeze, maybe, from a closed window, or an itch on my leg that I couldn't explain, I'd go to my desk and write another poem, make another phone call.

And then one night, after I'd tucked my brother in, I lay in bed and listened with my hands over my ears to my mother throwing up in the bathroom. A very strange thing happened right then. I saw two figures standing in my closet among my jackets. They were of average size and stood stock-still. They seemed to be waiting for something, though what, I didn't know. They stayed there in the shadows, just out of reach of the pool of light that spilled across my carpet from my window and the street outside—they stayed there, motionless, for probably ten minutes, and then, without warning, they disappeared.

I knew that this—whatever it was—was extremely significant, the sort of occurrence, the sort of *sign*, that would be a sin to ignore. I went down into the garage and got my dad's ladder and I carried it three blocks to Emily's cul-de-sac and into the backyard of the house facing hers. I set my ladder up on the back patio and looked through the sliding glass doors where a man and a woman were sitting on their couch in a brightly lit room watching television. I climbed the ladder, slowly and very softly, and I crawled up the slope of the roof to the top of the V, and then I scooted down the other slope on my backside, inches at a time, until I was at the edge, facing the empty street and Emily's house, and then, very carefully, I put my toes against the gutter and stood up. I yelled Emily's name until her light went on. She opened the window and put her head out.

"I'm going to jump!" I said. "I mean it!"

"Don't!" she said, "Don't!" and she left the window. More lights turned on inside. I opened and closed my hands. I cleared my throat and waited. It was an overcast night and I was sweating. In the time between coming up with the idea in my room and actually climbing up onto the roof, I'd become very fright-

ened. My legs were shaking and they'd been shaking for a long
time. I had a strange feeling in my stomach that was beyond
simple fear, something much more solid, and I was afraid it
would make a sudden lunge and carry me over the edge with it.

People were beginning to come out of their houses and
gather in the street. Emily ran out in a pink bathrobe with her
parents close behind. I came close to falling off the roof right
there.

"What are you doing here?" she said. There was something
very fearful in her voice.

"Nothing," I said. My own voice was shaking like crazy.
"You look nice."

"Don't move!" her mother said. "Don't move!"

The crowd was getting bigger. The man and the woman
who'd been watching television came out and stood in the
middle of the street, staring back at their house, confused and
disoriented. I had a strange feeling right then. All those people
in the street—I didn't know them and had never seen most of
them before—but I missed them terribly.

"Someone's coming to get you down," Emily's mother said.
"Just stay where you are."

"I didn't know it was this high," I said.

I stayed exactly where I was. I waited, and shortly the police
came and a fireman climbed up after me and backed me down.
It took a long time.

The cops had me sit in their squad car while they talked
to Emily and her parents, and then they got in and drove me
toward home. I turned around and looked through the rear
window as we pulled away and I saw Emily and her parents
walk back toward their house, her dad's hand on her back, and
then Emily, before going in herself, turned for a second, and
watched us drive down the street. There was something very
touching and romantic about that. I put my hand up to the
glass, like I'd seen in a movie. It was a movie where a fugitive

had been caught after a chase that had lasted thousands of miles, across every ocean in the world, and his girl tore her clothes and wept and fell to the ground as they drove him away from her. I turned around in my seat and listened. The cops warned me to stay away from Emily. They said her parents were going a little bit crazy with all of this, her dad especially, and it was time I stopped what I was doing for everyone's sake.

I warned them about my mother before we got to the door. I said she'd been suffering from a bout of tinnitus and wasn't feeling herself. She probably wouldn't say anything, I said, and she didn't. She sat on the couch while they explained everything, her neck craned back against the cushion, and she stared at the quiet television, sipping from a glass. I sat in a chair and looked from the cops to my mother and back again. I nodded my head to seem agreeable. After they finished, they thanked her for listening, and then they took me outside to the front porch and told me they were going to send someone from an agency to come and see us, but I assured them that everything was fine. "She's not always like this," I said. "She's just not feeling well tonight." And besides, I told them, my dad would be home any minute.

When the cops drove away I went inside and stared at the television. A strange-looking man ran into an enormous church. Suddenly a brilliant light poured through the stained-glass windows and flooded the church. The man's face was filled with the light. It seemed like an odd idea for a movie. I checked to see if my mother was watching but she wasn't. Her eyes were closed and her head was tilted back against the cushion.

"This is a weird movie," I said.

I began fooling around with a glass bird that had been on the lamp table for as long as I could remember. I stuck it to my forehead and moved it around my face. "I don't know who those guys were," I said. "I think they were Jehovah's Witnesses."

She didn't laugh so I kept talking. "I wasn't trying to kill myself," I said. I felt the bottoms of my shoes with my hand. The man on the screen ran to the pulpit. He looked like he was shouting. Something bright flew in through one of the windows. "I don't know what I was trying to do," I said. "I thought it would just be me and her."

I went upstairs and lay on my bed. I watched my fish swim around above me. I felt very lonely. I kept picturing Emily looking back at me from her doorway as the police car pulled away. There were tears in her eyes. I sat down at my desk and wrote a thirteen-page poem about a man in a wheelchair who falls for a young blonde maiden, only to be hit by a semi as he rolls across the street toward her house. This one I seemed to mean more than the others. I put it in an envelope, wrote Emily's name on it, and delivered it to her mailbox before school the next day.

A few days later, Emily's mother called and invited my parents and me over to their house. That afternoon I'd received the letter from the school in Nebraska asking me to come. I was flattered that they wanted me and felt a little bad that I'd have to reject their offer. For this reason, and Emily's mother's invitation, I was in a definite whistling mood. I put on my dad's suit and slicked my hair back, then walked over. It was a warm night and I liked listening to the clopping sound my shoes made on the sidewalk, and the somewhat mythical tones I could make with my whistle. I waved to cars and made clicking noises at any animals I walked by.

I explained, when I got to the house, that my parents had been unexpectedly called away on business but that they sent their regards, and Emily's mother led me to a chair in their very large living room. She stood leaning against one wall and I sat on the chair facing Emily's dad, running my finger over my eyebrows nervously. The house was a palace, high ceilings and paintings of little kids on the walls.

"Well?" he said.

"It's nice to be here, sir," I said. I looked around. "So this is what it looks like from the inside."

"Why don't you tell me why you won't leave my daughter alone," he said.

"Excuse me?" I said.

"You heard me."

"I do leave her alone."

"I'm afraid you've got that wrong there, pal," he said. He seemed much larger than he had two nights before. He was losing his hair at the front and it made him look mean. I noticed his hands were clenched like he had bottle caps in them and was trying to imbed them in his palms. I did that quite a bit, myself.

"I'm afraid I don't understand," I said.

"I don't know where your parents are, but let me tell you something," he said. "I want to make it clear to you that this is your last warning. If you come within ten feet of her, I'll call the police. Quit calling, stop writing, and stop all your little fucking pranks. You're going to get yourself killed," he said. "Take that however you want."

I thought this one over while I rubbed my eyebrow. I was confused about the direction the conversation had taken. I wondered if Emily was upstairs. Her mother came and sat down next to her husband and leaned forward toward me. Her arms were crossed in front of her stomach and they pushed up her breasts. She had the same green eyes as Emily, the same color cheeks.

"Will," she said. "You're not acting normal."

"I *am* acting normal," I said.

"No," she said. "You're not."

"I *am*," I said.

"*No. You're not.*"

"This is just a bit off-setting, Mrs Swanson," I said. "I have to admit I thought we were going to talk about something different."

"Will," she said. "Listen. You've got to stop harassing Emily."

I looked at Emily's dad. He was leaning back into the couch, very stiffly. "I'll certainly give it some thought," I said.

"You're a sick little fuck," he said.

"Frank," his wife said.

"You don't have to insult me, Frank," I said.

But Frank was riled up. He opened his hands wide. He leaned forward and pointed a finger at me. "Look you little faggot," he said, but he didn't finish. He got up suddenly and went into the other room. He walked over to the bar against one wall, and very loudly, began pouring himself a drink.

I looked at Emily's mother for a second. She was looking into the other room, where her husband was. She seemed very concerned about him for some reason. I looked at him too.

"She's sleeping with Jim Pierce, you know," I said. "They do all sorts of sick things together. I'm just telling you."

The glass dropped. Her dad came running at me. I saw it coming too late and by the time I did see it, I tried to brace myself against the couch cushion, I tried to turn away, but by then he had reeled back and knocked me across the side of my face. There was a pop and the world went blue. I rolled off the couch and onto the floor. I held my jaw in my hand. There was a loud, high-pitched ringing sound, and I blinked my eyes to keep from losing consciousness. I may have, actually, for a second or two. Then I was on my back, looking up at the ceiling. My soul was about to leave my body; I could taste it in my mouth. I put my finger to my lips and it came back red. Two people were yelling at each other. I made a noise in my chest and in my throat, the sound of confusion.

Emily's mother was kneeling over me.

"God, he's bleeding," she said. "Get a towel!"

"What?"

"Frank! Get him a towel! For *Christ's sakes!*"

"I'm leaving," he said. And he left.

Something strange was happening and I began to panic. My muscles contracted, my body stiffened, my arms stuck to my sides. "I can't move," I said. "I can't move!" I coughed into the carpet, rocking back and forth on my side. Things felt like they were tearing. I couldn't move and I kept yelling that I couldn't and Emily's mother kept yelling at me that I was fine.

"You can *move!*" she said.

"I can't!" I said.

"Yes, you *can!*"

"*I can't!*" And I couldn't.

Of course, after a few seconds, I could. She gave me a bag of frozen peas to put on my face. I kept saying that I didn't know what had gotten into Frank. I stressed that I had just been sitting there peacefully, minding my own business. I wondered what my own dad was doing. I hadn't seen him in a long time. I wondered if Emily had heard all the commotion. Her mother helped me to her car, I put an arm over her thin shoulder for balance, and she drove toward home.

Now the world was veiled in blue and it was blurry. The lights in the houses seemed to pulsate rapidly. I could hear them moving, a very high-pitched whir, and I wondered if the crack in the jaw Frank had given me had somehow scrambled my frequencies. Some of these lights emitted a very faint but constant beeping sound that I could hear from the passenger seat.

"Can you hear that?" I said.

"I should probably talk to your mother," Emily's mother said.

I didn't think this sounded like a good idea.

"She's asleep," I said. "I'll tell her about it tomorrow. We probably won't sue."

We didn't have peas, so I took a bag of corn from our freezer and iced my jaw on the bed. My angelfish floated quietly in her corner of the tank. The feeder fish swam around and bumped into one another. The bruise on my chin had turned into an almost breathtakingly beautiful swirl of blue and pink and gray, but it was killing me. I closed my eyes and had a dream.

The dream was based on an actual event that took place when I was six years old and my parents and I were having a picnic one evening on Dash Point Beach, a small state park on the Puget Sound. While we were there, a boy tried to swim out to a buoy. He didn't make it. He drowned. We heard his mother standing far away on the edge of the water—the tide was out—she was crying out, *My baby! My baby!* over and over again. Her voice was sorrow and it filled the sky. We packed our things and left, drove home.

This is what happened, as well as I can remember it. But in the dream I had that night, I wasn't six, I was almost eighteen, and sitting alone on the beach except for the woman, the boy's mother, who was on her knees in the distance, at the waterline, crying out desperately, and two dark figures, who had come to stand on each side of her. They were stooped and whispering in her ears.

Then from far out, a mile maybe, under a red, sunless sky, the drowning boy's hands shot up above the water. I saw this from my place on the beach. I stood and attempted to shout toward the woman and the two figures with her. I jumped up and down and waved my arms. I tried to let them know that he was still out there, that he needed help, but no noise came from my mouth, and the louder I tried to shout, the more silent I seemed to become—or, the more silent I seemed to *feel.* I picked up a rock from the sand and threw it. Then I was an arm's distance away from him, hovering over the water. The boy was writhing around in it, gasping for breath. He pulled his shoulders up and pressed his hands down against the surface, trying to lift his body over the waves. The woman was shout-ing, *My baby!* and I could tell that in the midst of everything that was happening, in the midst of his trauma, in the midst of everything, the boy was hearing it. I could tell he was hear-ing it because the more the woman shouted, the more franti-cally he tried to stay above the surface. Then there was another sound, a loud and violent creaking, and the sky was coming off its hinges—that's the only way to describe it—swinging back and forth, about to give way. The woman had now collapsed on the sand and the two dark figures looked out over the Sound at me, at the boy—the boy's shoulders sank—I was pulled away— and then the sky crashed down over everything.

Noise from the street woke me up. Glass breaking and a series of thuds. I lay still for a second and then I got up and ran to the window. A man jumped into a big white car in the middle of the street and quickly drove away. I stuck my head out and tried to see the license plate, but he was driving too fast. He went around the corner and was gone.

I grabbed my notepad, put on my jacket and went downstairs. The television was on with the volume turned up loud. My mother was passed out on the couch. Her mouth was open and she was snoring. She looked uncomfortable. I put my hand up to my jaw. It ached.

My little brother put his head over the railing and looked down onto the living room.

"What is it?" he said.

I looked up. "Nothing bad happened," I said. "Go back to bed."

"I heard something."

"It was just the wind. Go get in bed."

"Is Mom all right?"

"She's fine," I said.

I turned the volume down and went outside and walked out to the car. I looked at my house and at the houses down the block. Most of them were dark at this time of night. I looked at the sky, at the grass. I looked everywhere except in the direction of my mother's car. I didn't want to look at it until the last possible moment, but pretty soon my hands were against it, and I was forced to.

There were shards of glass and red plastic on the ground. Both rear lights had been knocked out. I wrote this in my notepad: *Both rear lghts out. Have been shattered.* I went around to the front, running my hand over the top. *Top DAMAGED*, I wrote. *Looks as if someone took heavy object and swung with grt. force. Paint and frame damage. Headlights out. Windshld and other mnr. structure damage.*

After I'd made my assessment, I walked back into the house, then straight into the garage and I picked up the first blunt instrument I could find, a shovel. I walked back through the house, past my mother and out the door, and I remember biting down hard on my teeth and squeezing up my face, closing my eyes tight, until they felt like they would pop. I made a high-pitched sound in the back of my throat, a sound that resembled a blender turned on and left on. I walked outside to the car, to the passenger door, and I swung the shovel as hard as I could. A terrible metallic sound fled down the street, through the rows of houses, and when I looked, the door was dented so totally I'd never get it open again.

I went inside and put a blanket over my mother and took her glass and put it in the dishwasher. I turned off the television and all the lights downstairs. I listened to her sleep for awhile. Then I went up into my room and on a piece of notebook paper I wrote a letter to the school in Nebraska, asking if they offered classes in fisheries. I told them I sincerely hoped that they did and that I would be waiting eagerly, on the edge of my seat, for their reply.

A few weeks later I graduated. I spent the summer mowing lawns around the neighborhood. My dad called one night and apologized for not making it to my ceremony. I hadn't gone myself, but I didn't tell him that. He said he was proud that I'd been accepted into the school in Nebraska and that he'd be honored to drive me. Since I hadn't yet figured out how I was going to get there, I told him I could cancel my plans and go with him instead, under the condition that he'd make sure my mother and my brother were taken care of and given regular meals.

One of the original five goldfish in my tank died around this time. There'd been no warning signs. They'd all seemed to be living normal and satisfactory lives. But one day I came home from mowing lawns and he wasn't in the mirror. I found him dried out and bug-eyed on the carpet below the tank—for some reason he'd jumped ship. I put him in a plastic film container and my brother and I held a service in the backyard. I said a few words and then we buried him about six inches beneath the beauty bark.

After a week of steady icing, my bruise went away, but I continued cold compresses for a few more days in case of long-term damage beneath the surface. I kept my mother's car parked on the side of the house and rarely drove it. Still, I washed it every Tuesday. I made sure the house was always clean and in good shape in case—although I never believed for a second it might happen—Emily might stop by one of these nights.

But she didn't and pretty soon it was time to go. The morning of our departure, I walked my brother to Winchell's and bought him breakfast. I told him everything I'd learned about the world, which wasn't much. People might let you down, I said, but don't let it worry you. You're not crazy, I told him. You're not even close to crazy.

I put my hand on his shoulder and told him he was the man of the house now, which meant he was going to have to take care of the old lady. He accepted this task with as much solemnity and tact as could be expected from an eight-year-old. He nodded his little head and took smaller bites from his doughnut.

My dad showed up at the house in the afternoon, and he and my brother loaded the car. I wandered around the living room picking up various things from various tables and inspecting them, and then I sat down across from my mother.

"I guess this is it," I said. I stood and stretched my arms above my head, then sat down again. "I don't have to go."

She stared at the television but she didn't seem to be watching it.

"You should open the blinds more," I said. I wanted to stay. Something told me that if I left now, everything would fall apart. Outside I could hear my dad and my brother laughing and loading the car, but in the living room it was so quiet I could hear my toes moving around in my shoes.

Then my mother did something uncustomary. She made a gesture that I would think about a lot from then on. I think about it a lot. She closed her lips tight and tilted her head. She ran her hand to the top of her head and took a handful of hair between her fingers and squeezed hard. She looked at me then, and there was something very sorrowful, very heartbroken and searching in her expression. That is to say, she was asking me—she wasn't saying anything—but she was asking me how things could have turned out the way they had, how what should have been such a pleasant life could have taken so many unfortunate turns, and it's occurring to me now—I almost shouldn't say it—that it will be difficult for me to ever love anyone more than I loved her right then.

But I didn't have an answer for her.

I stopped going to class after the second day. Fisheries 101, I found, was not the true source of all knowledge. The professor was interested in discussing ecosystems, water resources and pollution, river management, molecular genetics, marine environment, stock-separation techniques, and so forth. He was not interested, as far as I could tell, in answering the essential questions: why fish swim in schools, for example, or how they swim or breathe at all.

This was terribly disappointing. I stayed in bed the entire third day and didn't leave the basement. My cold sore was getting progressively worse, no matter how much Neosporin I put on it, and I suspected that some of my fellow students had been mocking my Band-Aid behind my back. These things put off my interest in the school's fisheries department, certainly, but above all—and this was important—there was no water in Nebraska.

I started spending my time in the student center drinking Cokes and playing pinball and video games, watching people bowl on the three-lane alley. One night I fell in with a group of cowboys who had come from an even smaller Nebraska town to take jobs in the school cafeteria, which was located in the same building. They needed an extra man for bowling and one of them asked me if I wanted to play. I said I did. I sat at the scorer's table and every time my partner would even glance a pin, I would congratulate him on a masterful throw and try to give him high fives. And I'm not saying there was anything special about these guys. They weren't even cool for cowboys. None of them had ever, as far as I could tell, been within ten feet of a girl, let alone touched a tit on a kiss goodnight as I had, and mentioned, a few times, to my partner. But human contact seemed necessary in maintaining one's sanity and, simply put, there was nowhere else for me to go. I was a terrible bowler and we lost. Afterward they all got in a car and left me in the parking lot to walk home in the dark.

An hour later I was sitting at my kitchen table drinking a

pop. People were yelling and laughing in the street outside. I went out, walked up the steps, over to the front porch and sat down. I put my head on my arms. I felt, I might have said, bound by sorrow. I missed my mother and my brother and my old man. Everything I'd said to him ran through my head and sunk me. I missed Emily. I went back down inside and took the Fish Bar flyer out from under the bed and my notepad and decided to call her. I would ask her to come to Nebraska and live with me. I would beg her to come. I would apologize for the terrible things I'd done. I would tell her I was in love with her. I would tell her my heart was breaking. I would get on my knees and tell her I was falling apart. I would say I couldn't live without her and she would tell me—I hoped she would tell me—that she'd been waiting for a long time to hear me say it like that, that she would be on the first plane in the morning.

She answered after the first ring. The television was going in the background. A crowd was laughing about something.

"Please don't hang up," I said.

"Not this again," she said.

"No," I said. "I'm not going to do anything."

"I'm getting my dad," she said.

"I'm not gonna do anything!"

"Please just leave me alone."

"Your dad punched me in the face," I said. I don't know why I mentioned this, other than she wasn't reacting to my call in the way I'd expected.

"I'm hanging up," she said.

"Let me ask you a question!"

"I'm hanging up. Goodbye."

"That's funny," I said. "That's a joke, right?"

"You need help," she said, and then she hung up.

"I do need help," I said. "I know it."

I put on my shoes and splashed my face with water. I put a fresh Band-Aid on my cold sore. Then I walked out into the darkness and got lost in it. I wandered toward the fields outside of town and then I wandered through them, down a series of narrow winding roads, not knowing where I was going, but thinking for some reason that what I needed to do was walk, or maybe that I needed to *start* walking.

I whistled, but just listening hurt my heart. I kept walking, and in rural towns, those roads can turn around on you and you can find yourself completely devoid of direction, and if you have never been good with direction in the first place, you can find yourself in a lot of trouble, which, after the third hour of wandering, I was ready to admit.

Because I had no idea where I was—I wasn't anywhere, really. The sidewalks had ended miles before and I'd kept telling myself that every marker I passed, a rock or a particular tree or a field where someone had dumped a big pile of cement, I kept telling myself that I recognized these things, that I remembered seeing them as my dad and I had come into town, so it was baffling, almost hurtful, that they hadn't led me anywhere.

Clouds had come and covered the stars; they had, it seemed, removed the sky. I'd walked out into the darkness and I was lost in it. I was alone in Nebraska. I wasn't studying fish. I wasn't going to class. I had no one who knew me by name. There was no one, even back home, who would have been happy to see me, say I walked into their house to say hello. My girlfriend, or the girl I *wanted* to be my girlfriend, had torn my heart in two. I missed my family terribly. I missed everyone. I wished we could all be together again.

The road forked and I stopped. The wind blew and the hills rolled away from the fences on either side. Two rows of radio towers stood off in the distance on the horizon, red lights blinking in separate rhythms. The Milky Way stretched behind them like a thin, tired cloud, like the rim of a great big bowl. It was an enormous universe. The wind was picking up. I was tired. My feet hurt. My shirt was wet. My jaw ached. I stared at the towers, at the lights. I watched them blink. And then I had a vision.

In the vision, I'm looking down on myself as if from a camera suspended above my head. It starts with a shot of the inside of my ear and then it slowly pulls back and I see my cheek and the side of my face and my closed eyes and my hair and my neck and soon I can see most of my body, I see myself, curled up on the side of a road with my head resting on my hands like someone either dead or asleep. My jeans are rolled up past my knees and my legs are bare. And as the camera pulls back further, higher, I see a car—a mid-eighties sedan, I think— idling quietly on the road beside me with its headlights on. Then the vision was over and I was left alone with the lights on the towers, blinking.

I didn't see any other option than to lie down. I curled up on my side in a patch of cool grass next to the road and put my head on my hands. I stayed there, eyes closed, listening, and waited.

Soon I heard a car approach and stop next to me. The doors opened. I felt two people come and stand next to me, one on each side. One of them bent down and said something in my ear that I didn't understand, and then softly, gently, removed my arms and my nose. The other pulled off my ears, then unzipped my pants and pulled off my dick. They bent down on either side of me and spoke into my ears, or what had been my ears—the holes that were there. They each said something that I didn't understand with voices I didn't understand, and my eyes filled and I started crying, because I knew something, or my heart knew something—or the *answer* to something, and when you know the answer, it hurts terribly.

They got back in the car, and then another door opened and someone else got out. He walked over to me. He crouched down next to me. He put his hands on my head. I kept crying and didn't think to stop. He spoke words over me, and then he moved his hands down to my feet and pulled my legs off.

I could feel my skin harden and emit a mucus membrane that covered up every hole—where my nostrils had been, the holes that were my ears, every opening but my mouth. My lungs tightened in my chest and shriveled up. I started gagging, my throat constricted, and I coughed my lungs up out of my mouth. I flopped in the grass, slowly at first, not breathing, and then with every second, more and more furiously, more violently and painfully, the sky and what was in it a blurry mess above my head, and I knew, I absolutely knew, that unless someone came and got me to water soon—within seconds—I would die.

A door closed and the car drove away. Soon I stopped, and lay still. The ground was hard beneath me. Something wet fell on my face. The sky opened, spread rain over all the ground.

Maybe not. But I remember clearly that it took awhile to recognize that I was there, somewhere, in-between.

I waited patiently for the Lord;
and He inclined to me, and heard my cry.
He brought me up out of the pit of destruction,
out of the miry clay...

PSALM 40:1–2

GRACE (SO LONG! PART II)

First, Helen's hands had begun hurting. It happened in the morning—and that night they hurt so badly that she called her daughter Mary. She could barely hold the phone. She was scared. Mary came and took her to the hospital. Helen didn't know what was wrong with her and none of the doctors knew either. Does she always look like this? they asked Mary and Mary told them, No. Helen was retaining water—in her hands, her arms, her face, her stomach. She lay in the hospital bed and listened to the people talking about her. They seemed very far away. She says she's very tired, Mary said, and she doesn't know why. We'll have to keep her for awhile, the doctors said. They gave her diuretics and pain pills.

And she was very tired. And she could barely keep her eyes open but she was aware that the walls were shifting. The light was on in the hallway, she could see a sliver beneath the door. If this is my time Lord, let it be quick. She didn't want it to take a long time. She'd seen many of her friends go slowly. She'd seen the way their bodies had failed them, slowly, the ways their minds had left them. She'd taken care of these friends of hers—

she'd brought them communion, taken them out on drives around the lake. She'd always prided herself on her resilience— she'd raised four children alone—lived on her own since Claire had left, thirty-five years ago—she'd worked at the library to support them, she'd retired, she went to Mass, drove her friends around. She'd had a blessed life. But if this is my time, Lord, let it be quick. I'm ready—someone was moving outside in the hallway. Or was there something else to do?

And weeks passed and Helen was still tired. Her hands hurt. She stopped taking the pills that made the walls move but even so, even without them, sometimes she would forget where she was, whom she was talking to. Come closer. I can't see you. The doctors said there wasn't anything more they could do—they'd done tests, made her as comfortable as they could. She shouldn't be alone in her condition, they said, and they sent her to live with Mary in Federal Way. Mary had always been a good daughter, a good friend—Helen was proud of all of them: Tom, Anne, Claire—but she hated to be an imposition. She told herself that if it wasn't going to be quick, then she would have to get better. In three weeks, she told them all, she would be back in her apartment in the city, back going to Mass every day, back taking care of her friends. Mary and Dick rolled her into the guest bedroom and lifted her into bed. They'd put flowers in a crystal vase on the nightstand. She had to go to the bathroom. How could she tell them?

When it would become unbearable and she'd have to take the pills that made her more tired, more confused, and the walls would bend—when the pain was too much—when she was afraid—when she still couldn't lift her legs or walk or go to the bathroom by herself—when she couldn't turn the pages of her Bible—when she missed Mass for the eighth week—when she couldn't remember the rest of the song she loved so much (it began:

This day God gives me strength of high heaven),

finally—although she told them all that she was going to get better—she had her children check her into St Joseph's Senior Care Center, and in all truth, though it was her own decision and the best one to be made, in all truth, it only seemed to make her more tired.

St Joseph's was in the city, closer to her friends, closer to her apartment, her car—and it wasn't like a hospital, *exactly*— they called it a home—there were lots of old people walking around—and the bed was comfortable, not as comfortable as her own in her apartment, of course—it wasn't a bad bed by any means—

But there was something else.

The black ladies were from Mississippi and they brought her meals and helped her with her wig and going to the bathroom. She hated anyone to see her like this, but they were humble people, themselves, and she tried to take it all with good humor, and she was too tired to take it with anything less. Helen didn't want anything in her room because she was going to go home soon. But Anne and Tom came one day and brought old pictures of the family, of Helen's husband and herself in front of the cathedral in St Paul, dried flowers, a painting of the Virgin from the dining room wall.

The doctors couldn't find what was wrong with her. Why do her hands hurt so much? Anne asked. What's going on inside her? None of them knew. They brought in specialists, looked in books. Helen forgot the beginning of the song one night and she listened to her heart beating in her ears for a long time, staring at the strip of light beneath the door, this other door (though it looked so much like the last one—and the room looked like—where was I then? Where is—) and she rang the bell, finally, when she couldn't be sure that she was breathing.

They took her back to the hospital. Don't fill the bed, Mary told the people at the home. They said they wouldn't.

She'll pass away within the year, the doctors said.

When her family visited, a nurse propped Helen up in her bed and Helen smiled and read the cards that said *Get Well Soon* and she thanked them, and smiled and listened to the news. She had grandchildren all over the country and a new great-grandchild was on the way—someone was getting married, she had the most difficult time figuring out who. Other things were happening and it was difficult to keep up—why was that? Why was she always so confused? She'd been ready. She hated for them to see her like this.

And wasn't it sad, really? Sad to not go quick?

Claire came to the hospital one afternoon and sat down next to her mother. She read aloud a section from a Trollope novel and when she had finished, Helen closed her eyes.

It's not that the road is steep, she said. It's that it's so long.

Claire listened and touched her mother's hand. She put the book on the bedside table. Her mother's eyes were closed tight and Claire could hear her breathing in short, quick bursts through her nose, her lips closed tight. Claire asked her Christ for the right thing to say. What *is* the right thing to say? What do we tell each other in these conditions? What do we say when we're falling apart?

You can go, Mom, Claire said. You know it's all right for you to go.

Helen didn't say anything for a time. Claire waited. Helen said:

I want to go. I'm afraid I can't. She looked into the dark. She began to cry.

Why can't you? Claire said.

Helen shook her head. She covered her face with her hands.

Why can't you go?

She didn't know.

Why do you think? Claire said.

I think— Helen said.

She thought she hadn't suffered enough.

You don't need to suffer, Claire said.

I haven't suffered. Not enough.

You don't need to suffer.

I do.

No, Claire said. You don't need to suffer. Not anymore.

They talked together more. They remembered things. Claire's father, Helen's husband; they remembered the good things. They remembered together, and finally, when it was getting late, Claire had to leave; she would come back tomorrow. She would read more Trollope. Open the curtain, dear, before you go. Claire walked to the center of the room and drew back the curtain between the two beds. The bed on the other side was empty now.

The nurse brought Helen dinner. Pulled back the blanket. Propped her up and put the tray on her lap, then left. Helen looked down at her plate. Chicken, mashed potatoes, carrots. She looked out the window, at the brick building across the alley, at the rows of windows. The sun was reflecting off the windows and she couldn't see inside, but that was all right. Something was happening. She began to breathe slowly. She began to relax. She felt a warmth [Back home in St Paul when she was a girl there was an old man who would bring ice on the back of his wagon and she would always stand inside at the door waiting for him and when he would pull up front, she would call her mother outside. Her mother would come out. How are you today, Mr Lawrence? How is your back today? and Mr Lawrence would say that it was fine, nothing to complain about—his wife was making ice cream to sell at Smith's, he had two boys off at college, a younger boy and a girl at home, terrors around the house. Mr Lawrence would bring the ice into the house and Helen would run ahead of him into the kitchen and he would strain under the weight—his back bent even when his arms were empty—and after he'd taken it down to the cellar and come up again, he would wipe the sweat from his brow and say to her mother, This one is growing so fast, and he would look at Helen kindly and she would feel heat in her cheeks and he would ask her questions—Are you ready for school? Are you ready to begin? and she would say, Yes, she was ready. She was reading on her own already, her mother had taught her, and after her mother had poured Mr Lawrence a glass of water and they had sat and talked about their children, about the town, about the church, Mr Lawrence would stand and say that he couldn't afford to dawdle and Helen would follow her mother and Mr Lawrence back through the house, and when she stepped through the door again, onto the porch and down onto the street by Mr Lawrence's wagon, she would be standing beneath an expanse of blue sky, and Mr Lawrence would say goodbye to the two of them, and she and her mother would stand in the street together, watching as the buggy turned the corner at the end of the street and disappeared. She would feel the heat and her mother would tell her to hurry back inside before she caught a stroke and then her mother would turn and go inside and she, Helen, would stand watching the space where the wagon had disappeared, fanning herself, and when she had finally turned, herself, to go back inside, she would feel an exquisite sense of the rightness of things, a sense of the fineness of things, the safeness of things, and she would not worry about Mr Lawrence or his bent back—she would not worry because why should she worry about Mr Lawrence when they shared so much and she would always see him tomorrow.] [Maybe she didn't need to after all.] surge through her. She felt it all over. It felt good. Through the window, a young man in the building next door was pushing a broom. [She could see

down, now, into the dark alley. She was very high.] She wondered if he was who she thought he was.

IT'S TAKING SO DAMN LONG TO GET HERE (VII)

If I had to try and make some sense out of it I guess I would have to say that I worry I'm going to be waiting so long I'll forget what I'm waiting for. Does that make sense? You worry you'll forget what you're waiting for and then you worry one day you'll forget that you are waiting for anything at all. Maybe you'll get up one day and go to work, and after work you'll come home and sit down in front of the TV, for instance. Or the radio or whatever. And you turn the volume down because all of a sudden you have the sense that *something's slipped your mind*. And you sit there and wonder about it for awhile, your interest is piqued, you know there's something...there's something, but what is it? And finally, you just shake it off. You turn the volume back up. You figure you must have just left something at work or forgot to pick something up from the grocery store, or something like that—something *trivial*. Surely nothing *important*. So you shake it off. But what it is—what it really is—and this is the part that gets to me when I start thinking about it—what it really is is this is the exact moment in your life that you've forgotten you're waiting for something.

So then, without even knowing it, this is when you've lost your hope.

LOOKING OUT
FOR YOUR OWN

Some things, you need to let go.
I've found this out the past few months. First it was my brother.
Then it was Shannon, my girlfriend and the only girl I've had
sex with. I know Shannon from school. I've actually known
Shannon since kindergarten. But we became friends when we
got to junior high and then high school came along and one
thing led to another, and pretty soon we're hanging out so
much it's like we're boyfriend and girlfriend, but without the
kissing or the sex. Then one night, when I took her out to
the pier to watch the water, I kissed her. I remember this well,
because I was real nervous about it. I thought, Once I kiss this
girl, I'm going to have to start knowing her very well. More
than I did, anyway. She was leaning over the railing and you
could hear the water bashing against the pillars below and
the creaking of the old wooden boards. She called me Drew,
as opposed to Andrew, which is more formal. I was standing
behind her about five feet away and all of a sudden she turns
around and just stares right at me. You should have seen it. It
was like the movies. The moon, which was above my left shoulder, was hitting her right in the face, turning her face all white,

and her hair, which looked gray but was really mahogany, was blowing all around her face and in the wind, like something was pulling her by the roots. And behind her, just the stark blackness of the ocean, which was amazing because of the way the moon hit her right in the face, like she was everything worth lighting up. She was wearing a blue sweater that hung kind of baggy on her, and blue jeans. She was also wearing black Converse All Stars, I remember. She just stood there and stared at me, like I said, and I knew, because she didn't say anything, just stared, that she wanted me to kiss her. So I walked over to her, and she put out her hands for me to take, and I took them, and then I leaned into her mouth and kissed her real soft at first, and she sighed, and then she opened her mouth and I opened mine and put my arms around her and held her close.

There are certain things about a person that you could never know. Why, for instance, a girl might cry sometimes when you're in bed together and you've just had sex and everything finally seemed to go well. But the next thing you know, she's crying and holding on real tight to your arm for no reason that she can explain. Or why some people might get violent all of a sudden, and come over to your house and bust down your door and the next thing you know, this guy's on top of you and he's got his hands around your neck squeezing so tight you can't breathe, and one side of your throat touches the other so you feel like you're going to throw up or pass out, and then you start worrying that this could be IT; "Curtains!" like they say. Then he gets up and walks out of your house, just like that.

You've got to ask yourself what really just happened and why, and the conclusion you must in the end come up with is because something must have happened to that person that's triggered by something that is right now happening. Something that they probably couldn't even explain if someone were to ask.

Probably what happened is some dirty old man (or it could be a woman, but mostly it's a man) put some moves on them when they were a tyke and it really gets to them still, when something makes them remember it. Or maybe their old man used to beat the shit out of them and they blocked it out, but some things just trigger it out of them, so they're doing the same thing. This is called Repressed Memory Syndrome. It's also why some girls dress up in all black and paint their faces white, like death, and put black around their lips and eyes, like death. It's also why some guys walk around pretending like they're girls, and walking like them and talking all feminine, and sometimes when you go to the city, they're walking around together and holding hands and giving you hard looks like you look at girls. It's most probably because they've got Repressed Memory Syndrome, which can only be cured by a shrink with psychotherapy. What they did for all that time before they had psychotherapists, I have no idea. I know they had perverts and assholes back then. Maybe they just dealt with it or maybe there wasn't a cure so some girls would grow up and cry whenever they'd be in bed with their husbands because they knew it reminded them of something real sinister but what they didn't exactly know, so the husband, who was probably a nice guy himself, would have to rub her hair and shush her back to sleep and blow on her forehead to make her feel safe.

As far as what guys would do—and not all of them turn out to be fags, by the way—they'd probably just have to keep a stiff upper lip and try to walk tall and forget about it, which is all right, I guess, for guys, because they are naturally tougher and, as my old man says, resilient.

This would have made no sense to me last year, but now, after everything that happened with Shannon and her dad, it's completely logical. You've got normal people like Shannon, and you've got crazy people, like Shannon's dad. Except while Shannon is normal in most respects, there are things about her that don't add up, that *aren't* normal, but they're so far different from the things that aren't normal about her dad, they're minor in comparison, or if not minor, then less dangerous at least.

I'm no expert on sex. I've only been with Shannon, and we've had actual sex less than ten times. The first time was maybe a year ago at my house when my parents first went away for the weekend. They do this a lot since my brother got sent away. This was the summer I turned sixteen and we'd tried to do it earlier, it's just that it never worked out. The first time we saw each other naked was in the front of my 1984 Toyota Corolla. Shannon took off all her clothes and I took everything off but my shirt—I'd gotten too tall too quick and I was worried I was way too skinny for a girl to want to look at—and we kissed and fooled around with each other's bodies, but when it came down to it, I was, as they say, impotent. I couldn't get it up to save myself, no matter what Shannon did to me or no matter who I imagined Shannon was instead of herself. I felt all embarrassed and I made a joke about it, and laughed and Shannon laughed too but it was hard to believe that she was laughing at my joke and not at me. She told me that it happens to every man some time or another and that made me feel a little better about the whole ordeal. Besides, she knew I'd been tired with school and working so many hours for the lawn service, and that cramped car was not very comfortable for my six-foot-four-inch frame.

When it came to sex, Shannon was usually the one to start it, more than me because after that first attempt I was pretty timid. I went to the library and I sat there one Saturday when I was supposed to be at work, looking through psychology books, trying to find out what's the cure for being impotent with a girl, when you used to get hard just thinking about her. I read up on the subject, but none of the books had any real advice and I felt embarrassed if anyone saw me reading sex manuals and Sigmund Freud. Shannon was usually the one to start it, but like I said, afterwards she'd sometimes cry and hold on to me tight. I'd tell her to hold on as tight as she wanted and, to take the sting out of whatever was hurting her mind, I'd tend to hold on to her too. When we finally did have sex, after a bunch of embarrassing attempts, it was that first time my parents left for the weekend. They hadn't been anywhere just the two of them since before I was born and my brother, who's three years older than me and mentally disabled, or retarded, had just gone to live in a home about two hours away. My mom was real broke up about it. We dropped him off at the home—it was sort of like a hospital, except that on the outside they had gardens and yards and people walking around—and the fact that it was more like a hospital scared my mom really bad, and she started crying and getting all hysterical, probably with guilt, and she started kissing Joe on the head and saying "My baby" over and over. This sent him into a crazy rage. My brother is six inches shorter and fifty pounds heavier than me. My dad had to man-handle him to the ground along with some help from a hospital employee, while my mom bawled into the arms of a nurse and I just stood there quietly, wondering if I'd ever have sex with Shannon and if we'd ever get married and if so, if we had kids, would any of them look like Joe. They had him on the ground with his hands behind his back screaming, and they dragged him that way, screaming, down the longest, narrowest hallway you've ever seen and this echo hit me, even when they were out of sight, this echo that raced down to the end of the hallway and back at me again, that sounded like a rat on fire, screaming for his life.

That's what I told Shannon that night at my parents' house, that he had screamed like a rat on fire, and she stared at the ceiling and finished puffing down the last of the cigarette I gave her. We were in my bed and we were both naked and I was amazed at the whole feeling of being locked up in sex, but that amazement that I had in me, and that relief also, gave way to guilt as all I could think of afterwards, as we lay there next to each other, was that look on Shannon's face when I finally managed to get inside her, and my brother being dragged down the hallway like a rat on fire, and my old man with sweat dripping down his forehead from wrestling his retarded kid to the floor—but Joe was a man now wasn't he?—and a dazed look on his face like, "My God, what have I done?" as if he had doomed the world to some terrible fate, and maybe he had. At least his world. "You've got to look out for your own," he used to tell me when I was younger and embarrassed to be seen with my brother. You couldn't reason with Joe, there was no order to his mind, it was all scattered and jumbled and chaotic. You had to walk on eggshells. He'd freak out on you, then he'd look at you like he'd never seen you before. "Don't do this. Don't do that," my mom would say. "No loud noises, don't touch him, but don't make him feel unwanted," because she knew, or she thought, that underneath his dumb ugly look, he knew exactly what was going on, and he had order in his mind. But my dad would say, "Look out for him, Andrew. He's your brother. He's family," and I know he was thinking of this as he watched them drag my brother off, kicking and screaming, and as he took my mom out of the arms of that nurse and as they walked away to fill out paperwork, forgetting about me, still staring down that empty hallway, where my brother had disappeared.

The lights were off but the curtains were open and Shannon had the covers pulled over her chest, and in the moonlight one side of her face was in shade, but the one closest to me was lit in white, and her skin looked china white and her mahogany hair looked gray. I talked for a long time more about Joe and the trip to the home and how my parents didn't say a word the whole trip back, because I didn't want to get to the real issue or I didn't know how to get to the real issue, and that was: why after all this time of wanting to make love to a girl, why could she only cry afterwards and hold tight to my arm like she was sad or afraid, or was remembering something, or knew there was something that she *couldn't* remember. We smoked cigarettes and looked at the walls and at the crosses made of shadows on the ceiling and I kissed her on the forehead, which was very warm and smelled like something I couldn't put my finger on (and still can't). Then I said, "Did it hurt?" and she nodded her head and I thought she might cry again but she didn't. And I was suddenly sickened by myself and I wanted to crawl away from her and hide in a corner or run from my own house, because I was so ashamed of myself and I thought about sex and the act itself, and really, what a horrible fucking thing it is. But then she said, "That's not why I was crying. I don't know why I was crying but not because of that," and then she kissed me on the chin.

This put me at ease a little, but we didn't have sex again for two months after that and it took even longer for her to lose that scared, painful look on her face those times we would do it, and the way her body would tense up and she'd clutch the sheets as if she was afraid if she let go, she'd go hurtling through the roof and lose her place on earth, sort of the same way my brother had when they dragged him down that narrow hallway. And it's right now occurring to me that your brain is like that hallway and it's so easy to go hurtling down it and it takes such an effort to fight against it, and it takes more than only someone next to you who'll let you hold them and tell you what everyone wants to hear, that everything will be all right.

I'd tell her this when she'd cry or when she'd wake up from a bad dream. Everything will be all right. But being how we are, and how two people can be completely different, no matter how they fit together, and no matter how many times you tell someone that everything will be all right, things aren't always all right.

Sometimes I'd get very quiet and Shannon would make every effort to get me talking. She'd ask me what's on my mind, and I know she was only trying to do what I did for her and that is to simply *be there* for her, to be someone she could clutch or hold on to. But no matter how much I liked her, or even possibly loved her (or love her now for that matter), there was nothing she could do to put me at ease, and above all, to rid me of the weight in my head, to unclutter my mind. When I feel this heavy inside, I usually go down to the pier and stare off into the water, at night especially, when it's quiet and no one is around, and where the lights on the hills behind me light up where I come from, and the dark of the ocean lays out there like a calm blanket that I know nothing about. It's like the dark parts of my mind I can't put my finger on.

Why, for example, did I get so angry when Shannon would ask me too many questions and ask me about Joe and growing up when I didn't want to talk that way? And why do I have a feeling that my parents are so unhappy with their lives and with the two of us? Why do they need to get away? And the question I ask myself all the time is why, when I am so attracted to Shannon, why was it so difficult to have sex with her?

Because though I make it sound like it's no big deal sometimes, it'd take me such a big effort to make myself be able to get inside her. Sometimes it'd take hours, sometimes it wouldn't happen at all. Sometimes she would do everything she could to make me get hard and finally on those occasions where nothing happened, she'd collapse off of me and lay there exhausted from trying to get me going with her mouth, and while she couldn't see me, the whole time I've been staring up at the ceiling or at the roof of the car, biting my lip and tearing up in my eyes, trying not to make any noise, and I'm so frustrated and ashamed because I am a man and to make her do all those things just so we can be together, seems sickening and shameful. On the times where it would work (and this could be after hours, and me finally rubbing up against her like a fool and sometimes using my hand) she'd roll over onto her side, which is where we'd learned is the easiest way, and she'd help me in, and I'll feel like screaming, hoping I won't lose it and have to start again, so I'll go at it real quick, trying to get it over with, and poor Shannon has to feel all the aggression that's not meant for her at all, but for me, and I come very quick. Which is when, when it was over, she'd turn over and kiss me and sometimes cry and hold tight to me, because she remembers something, or nearly remembers something that's so painful she's got to hold on to me—who she says she loves—and convince herself that the two things, while they're the same act and probably feel the same to her too, have nothing in common.

My parents leave most weekends. My mom, who's been moping around the house in a funk since my brother left, cries when she thinks no one's around, and stares off through the walls when she thinks no one's looking. My old man has taken a different approach to dealing with the guilt. He yells at me for the slightest reasons, and sometimes takes to pushing me around.

Most weekends they drive two hours away to a motel called the Eight Arms in Port Townsend. The hospital where Joe is living at is nearby. They spend the weekends there. My dad sits around in the motel room all day, watching sports on cable and drinking beer, and my mom spends most of the days at the hospital, visiting Joe. At night, they mostly stay in, although some nights they go out to eat, and maybe a movie. Sundays at four, they pack up the van and drive back home.

Shannon would come over and stay with me on the weekends. I asked her once if her dad knew where she was and she gave me a look that made me stop right where I was at. More than once, she's come over with a new bruise on her face that I never tried to ask her about.

How different can two people be? Once, when we were alone and watching TV, Shannon said to me, "What one thing did you want more than anything when you were a little kid?— You know what mine was?"

"What?" I said.

"For my mom to come back to life and for my dad to die."

I held her closer and being resilient, didn't say anything, just took a drag off my cigarette and listened to her breathe off to sleep. I can't say it's the thing I wanted more than anything, but when I was little, I used to wish that my brother would die and that I wouldn't have to listen to him anymore, or see him, or smell him, and I wouldn't have to defend him to the neighborhood kids who used to make fun of him and me. Sometimes I would wish it was me who would die, because the thought of me actually wishing something like that on my brother was too painful to face, being a little kid, especially all the times my mom would work to convince me that he was just like me, but different, and that I really loved him very much.

On one of my trips to the pier a few months after Joe had been gone, I said out loud, "There's your subconscious, always fucking with you," because you know, there's just nothing there to be done, short of psychotherapy, and in most cases who would want to remember something so horrible? It probably goes like this: The doctor lays you down—let's use Shannon for an example—he lays Shannon down and he says, "You cry and clutch Andrew's shoulder after he finally manages to have sex with you. Let's find out why," and then he makes her remember every detail (the feeling, the smell, the size, the shape) of what I think happened to her and what she knows, but really can't remember. He opens up her subconscious and he drags her down that hallway, kicking and screaming like she's a rat on fire, and you know she doesn't want to see it, she can't bear to see it, and then he says, like it's a magic trick, "Done! That's what happened!" Sometimes I think we're bound by the parts of ourselves that we have the least control of.

My brother, who has the body of a man, wears extra large diapers because he shits himself. He doesn't walk either, it's more of a lunge like a claymation doll, and he spins his head this way and that, opens his mouth and spits out the craziest choking sound. He drools on himself and blows snot down his face, but my mom, up until the day we all drove him to the home where he now lives, would take him to the barber shop on the first Tuesday of every month, and buy him new clothes every September during the Back To School sales. She would also take him for walks on nice days, leading him along like she was the caretaker of the zombie division at the local zoo. Then there's my dad, who hardly ever came home until very late and couldn't be in the same room as Joe for ten minutes before he'd either start yelling at him or go storming out of the room; he'd tell me anyways, when the kids from our street would yell at me and I was tired of defending whatever smarts my mom claimed Joe had, "You've got to look out for your own! He's your brother! He's family!" But my dad works hard at a print shop for twelve hours a day; he got tired of coming home to a house that smelled like shit-filled sweatpants and the constant noise—the constant drooling, "Na! Na! Na! Na!" and the screeching and the times when Joe would start flailing around madly, trying to crush, batter and break everything within the circle of his outstretched arms.

One night I was watching TV and listening to my parents creak around in their bedroom through the ceiling. My old man came downstairs and sat next to me in front of the TV, and he handed me a beer and took a giant pull off of his and said, with a hand on his huge but strong belly, "We're taking your brother to a home. Someplace where they can take better care of him." He looked sad, but he looked angry too and I realized what it was that made Joe so difficult for him and for me also, and it was this: No matter how much we walked on eggshells or defended him, or tried to love him and to talk nice to him and clean him, no matter how much we did these things, Joe would never recognize us. He'd never be able to point to a picture of my dad's broad frame and fat stomach and recognize that it was his father, and he'd never be able to look at me, skin and bones, and know that I was his brother. We weren't *his* in the same way that he was *ours*. My dad looked sad and as he sat there, he looked sadder and sadder, until the angry part of his face left him completely. I didn't say anything. I didn't make a sound. I thought if I were to sigh or take a deep breath, that would somehow hold me responsible. I could've told him it was the wrong thing to do and maybe they wouldn't have sent him away, or I could've told him it was a good idea and maybe they would've felt better about it, but I just sat there, looking at the TV, holding this beer in my hand. After awhile he got up and went back upstairs, which was probably more to his liking, and now I could breathe again.

Shannon didn't tell me that she was pregnant. But she did tell me that she had an abortion, which is weird I guess. She never mentioned that she was pregnant even after she knew I'd found out, and I can't see the point in it except maybe she didn't want me to have to think about how it was I found out. We stopped having sex, and I didn't touch her. We went out to places and she still loved me and she probably still loves me, although we are broken up, and I probably still love her too.

What happened was her dad got a phone call from Dr Birch

at the clinic and Dr Birch told him that Shannon was pregnant. This goes against all sorts of confidentiality laws, I know, but what can you do? My parents had left for the weekend and I was watching a movie on TV called *Vertigo,* and I hear someone bust through my front door. It's a great big oak door so you can really tell when someone throws it open. It rattled the walls and I turned around in my easy chair and there's Shannon's old man, standing in the doorway with his arms out at his sides, but bent at the elbows all menacingly, and a crazy look on his face like he was a lunatic. I didn't say anything. I was so surprised and plus, he was my girlfriend's dad and what could I say? The next thing I know he's running at me, calling me all sorts of names, and I try to scramble away but Shannon's dad is as tall as me and built thick like my dad and he's fast, and he's on top of me in a second and he's got his hands around my neck and his hair is hanging down and he's choking me, I feel my throat collapsing so no air can get through and I'm thinking I'm going to puke or pass out, then I start thinking this could be IT, like I'm gonna die. The whole time he's calling me a skinny fuck and a faggot and he's talking about Shannon and using words like slut and bang and knocked up. Right when I think I'm really going to die, his hands get soft on my throat and he stands up and walks out like nothing happened, but I don't see him because I'm on my side, coughing and gasping for air and if you were there all you'd hear would be me on the floor coughing, and the movie on the TV, and me bawling my eyes out for a very long time.

I didn't call Shannon although I wanted to. I was sure she was getting a beating at her house, but I didn't call her. I wanted to get my dad's gun and go over to her house and knock on the door and when that crazy fucker answers, to blow his brains out, or at least to go get her and drive her away from that lunatic. But life isn't a movie and I'm not heroic. I wish I was but I'm not.

I didn't tell my parents but what does that matter? My parents drive off to the Eight Arms Motel almost every weekend. My dad watches the Raiders or the Lakers or the Kings or the Dodgers, and my mom has grown tired of having no one to tend to during the weekdays and so she waits for the weekends and walks down that narrow hallway to my brother's room on Saturday and then again on Sunday and so everything's all right.

Shannon was laying in bed next to me with all her clothes on recently. She told me her dad made her have an abortion and now the baby that was inside her, now is dead. How about that?

"What are you thinking about?" she said.

I was staring up at the ceiling and I was watching the shadows from outside move around in the wind and it seemed to me that what we need most isn't to be comforted or assured, or told that everything will be all right. What's the use of crying and holding on to each other and talking in soft, soothing voices (or even asking each other what we're thinking about) when what we need is really something different and that is just to be saved.

This was our last night together. I broke up with her not because I didn't like her, or didn't love her, and not because I was afraid of her dad or anything. There are certain things that I do well and certain things that I can't do at all, no matter how much I wish I could. I can clean shit from between a grown man's legs and I can blow on a girlfriend's forehead and shush her to sleep. I'm excellent at comforting and trying to understand, and cleaning things up. But I'm no hero, as I said before. I'm too tall and too skinny and there's no meat to me. I can't put up a fight and I crumble when someone comes to threaten me; I can't even run away right. And I looked over at Shannon and at all the soft and smooth places on her face where there had been bruises that now had disappeared and I thought that my main problem is I can't look after my own. I really can't.

Afterwards I was alone in my bed and I was bored, so I got up and drove to the pier. No one was around, it was quiet. I looked out at the dark water and the lights on the hill behind me, and I listened to the sound of the water bashing up against the pillars and the creaking boards. There's another clinical term called catharsis. It's when everything inside you that you keep all bottled up just explodes right out of you, sort of like my brother screaming down that hallway or Shannon's dad choking me—except those aren't real good examples—one was just the standard reaction of a fucked-up brain and the other was just rage, pure and simple. There was no one around and it was quiet and I thought this would be a good time for it, for catharsis, to just let everything out. But you can't wish these things to happen, you can't just yell, you've got to wait until it bursts right out of you. Some people just stay the same, just like there are certain things about people that you could never know, just like some things you find you need to let go. So I leaned over the railing and I collected all the saliva in my mouth, and I leaned over and let the spit just sort of fall out of my mouth into the black water below, and I thought, "Curtains," not like it was all over, but like it was just the end of one act in a life that should take you past a whole lot more.

There is one last thing that I should mention about me and Shannon, and then it's all over and I can put it behind me. It was that first time I ever kissed her (and did I mention that I had never kissed a girl before that night?). In fact, we'd just finished kissing for probably twenty minutes, just kissing each other, then she'd rest her head on my chest and I'd put my chin on her head, then we'd kiss some more. It was on the pier. We'd just finished kissing when I took a step back and I looked at Shannon and there she was, like they say, "caught in the moonlight," in that blue sweater of hers. She catches her eye on something and she bends down and comes up with two rocks, the kind that fit perfectly in the palm of your hand. She hands one to me and she takes hers and she walks over to the edge of the pier and with a sly grin, she throws it as far as she can, and because it's so quiet, what you hear is a little, plunk! not too far off. And now I guess it's my turn, so I walk over and I start my windup, and I get my whole body into it and I swear I throw that rock so far, you never heard it come down. It just disappeared. All you could hear was the sounds of the waves splashing against the pillars and the pier creaking, and Shannon breathing, just breathing.

THOUGH OCCASIONALLY GLARING
OR VIOLENT, MODERN COLOR
IS ON THE WHOLE
EMINENTLY SOMBER:

THE BORDER

There were a lot of things that Robert couldn't remember, isolated things, pieces of the past of the present that were lost to him. It worried him sometimes, because you didn't always know just what it was you didn't remember. When he showed up to the site and no one was there, he figured everyone was late. The guys were always coming in late but Mike, his foreman, was always early and even Mike wasn't there. Robert sat for half an hour in the backhoe, waiting, smoking cigarettes as the sun rose. He was glad to have the extra time to rest; his back and his head were killing him and the arthritis in his hands had been bad lately. He was glad for the extra time, but he was a worker, after all, and before too long he walked across the street to the pay phone and called Mike.

Where is everybody? Robert asked. I'm down at the site.

What are you talking about? Mike said. I gave everyone the day off.

That's right, Robert said. He laughed. I must have forgotten. My mind's in bad shape.

He went home. Ruth was in her bathrobe making Amy's lunch. I got the day off, he said.

Good, Ruth said. We can spend the day together.

Robert walked into the living room. He sat down on the couch, turned the TV on.

Some things he never forgot. He never forgot his anniversary or Amy's birthday. His ideal fighting weight: 160, though he'd fought (and lost) at 168. Or his record: 146–158. He didn't remember many of his fights, but he knew his record. What if he forgot that too? Maybe it would be better that way.

He remembered that kid, Pierce.

Pierce wasn't a good fighter. He was young and inexperienced, hadn't known what he was doing. Robert had punished Pierce in two different fights, put Pierce out in twenty-seven seconds the first time. Pierce was nineteen or so, and Robert had been in his early thirties then. The second time, a few months later, Pierce lasted almost all three rounds before they called the fight. Robert had hurt the kid the first two and in the third round he kept it up, and Pierce wouldn't go down and Robert had kept punishing him with rights while Pierce bounced against the ropes, smiling out of his headgear, his arms down at his sides, wouldn't go down, couldn't hit back or wouldn't hit back and Robert, finally, had stopped. He put an outstretched left beneath Pierce's chin to hold him there, against the ropes, and with his right, Robert waved the ref over to stop the fight.

He remembered the ref that night was an old fat guy, bald head, mustache, flat nose, a nose like the one Robert had now, the bridge beaten down, flat and wide, the point at the bottom sticking out a bit. Pierce had had a hand in that during their third fight, which Robert had come into out of shape; he'd put on weight, he was smoking again, his lungs full of phlegm, and he remembered being tired before that fight, having worked a double shift the day before. Pierce had come running at him and Robert, whose strategy was to attack first and try to knock a guy down, had stumbled backwards, trying to block, but he wasn't a good blocker, or a good boxer, even; he was a big hitter, a powerful puncher, or once had been. And he lost this one to Pierce. He didn't remember much about it. He didn't remember going down or what happened after he went down. But he did remember being surprised by the kid, backing up, caught off-guard by the uncharacteristic offensive attack. And he remembered being back at work the next day with a splitting headache, his nose having been drilled back into his skull.

That had been his last fight, a first round loss. He lost a lot of money on himself, that fight. Amy was just beginning to walk then and he'd promised Ruth that this would be his last. He would quit and having already beaten Pierce twice, he put five hundred dollars on it, all the money they had, a straight-ahead odds-off bet with a man he didn't know, a friend of a friend. The money mattered then; it didn't matter anymore. And his record was lousy and even if he would have won that last fight, his record would still be lousy. But if he would have won that fight, he'd have gone out a winner, and that would have been something, at least.

He'd always wanted another shot at the kid. Come out of retirement. Tell Ruth he was going to the bar, fight, explain what needed explaining when he got home. But after that third fight, Pierce had disappeared. Robert would often check the local sports section, looking for news of the kid. Sometimes he'd go down to the Tacoma gym and ask around, but the few that even remembered the kid didn't know what had happened to him.

In yesterday's paper Robert had seen that Pierce was dead. Twenty-six years old. No mention of how he died.

He remembered the figure in the photograph. They'd used a boxing photo. The kid had his hands up, leaning forward slightly, knees bent, light on his feet, ready to deliver a combo.

Robert watched the news, smoking, remembering, until he

heard Amy talking to her mother in the kitchen and he put his cigarette out. Come give your old man a kiss, he called to her, and she came over and pecked him on the cheek. She was going to be eight on December sixteenth. Have a seat, he said, and she jumped up onto his lap—a *twinge* in his back. She put her arm around his neck.

What's the date today? he said.

The nineteenth, she said.

What month is it? he said.

November.

I know what month it is. Your old man's just messing with you. He faked a right to her stomach and she smiled, making no effort to block it.

Ruth came out with a sack lunch. We're late, she said. Get your jacket and jump in the car, and Amy jumped down from her father's lap, ran to the closet by the front door and put her jacket on.

She's been on that computer all morning, Ruth said. Now she's gonna be late. She walked to the entryway. What do you want to do today? she asked Robert. She was putting on her coat, over that old worn out green bathrobe.

I don't know, Robert said.

You haven't had a day off in a long time.

I know.

I'm supposed to go help out at the church today, but maybe we could go for a drive instead, she said. We haven't had time together in a long time. I'll have my mom pick Amy up after school.

OK, Robert said. Amy was struggling putting on her backpack. The thing must have weighed fifty pounds.

Tell that teacher of yours not so much homework, he said. You're gonna get a hernia.

OK.

You still the smartest kid in class? he asked.

Yes, Amy said.

Of course she is, Ruth said.

Then she put her hand on Amy's head and guided her out the door. Robert reached for his cigarettes.

Tom and Anna waited for the aisles to clear and then they stood and slowly walked toward the back of the church. Anna blotted at her eyes with a tissue. She always cried in churches, what was it that made her cry every time she was in one? She'd always been like this. Especially when they played music. The music today had been beautiful, so sad, and she had cried, but she would have cried even if the music had been happy, even if the occasion had been a happy occasion, even if she wasn't there to show her last respects to Tom's brother, Jim. She wished she hadn't cried, people must have thought she was faking it—she'd cried harder and louder than anyone, even her mother-in-law. They didn't know that she always cried in church.

Tom and Anna followed the crowd to the foyer and out and across the courtyard and into the building next door. There were tables set up with little sandwiches and cans of pop. She held on to Tom's hand.

I always cry in churches, she said.

I should go check on my mom, Tom said, and he let go of Anna's hand and walked across the room to where his mother was standing, surrounded by a group of women, her friends and sisters. Anna looked around—the room was crowded, and it was a small room—she sat down in a chair against a wall, looked at people in line for food. How could they eat at a time like this? She wasn't hungry, was never hungry.

She took a deep breath and stretched her back. So uncomfortable. Anna hated funerals. She hadn't been to many, but she hated them. She loved churches, though. She loved churches but couldn't go in one without crying. She figured she'd cry if she went to Europe and went on one of those tours of those old cathedrals. She'd follow the tour, past statues and stained glass, past lit candles and altars and she would weep and everyone would think she had problems. What's her problem? What's she crying about? The tour guide would say, *Ma'am, are you all right?* and the nicer ladies in the group would gather around her and rub her back and she would feel so embarrassed and alone, she would try to tell them, I always cry in churches, it's not anything, it's just a reaction, I'm fine. Then she would be too embarrassed because she probably wouldn't be able to stop crying even then and she'd have to leave, someone would try to follow her, she might even have to run from them, run out of the church, run down the steps and into—

But where was Tom? Wouldn't Tom be there with her? What was she doing in Europe without Tom? What the hell was wrong with her? Of course, Tom would be there with her. He was her husband.

She remembered the time Tom was gone on a fishing trip and she'd gone over to his mom's house and his mom had cooked a meal and Jim was there and she and Jim had been drinking—when was that? A year ago? Two years? How old was she now? Old. Too old. Concentrate. I'm twenty-nine years old. Twenty-nine years old. Almost thirty. Boo-hoo. She and Jim got drunk together and laughed together and her mother-in-law kept shaking her head at the two of them, not understanding young people, that was how she put it, and Jim wouldn't let her drive home because she was too drunk and she never got drunk, she always took care of her body, but that night she'd let loose a little bit and Jim took her home, and at home they drank the rest of Tom's scotch, and she felt so comfortable with Jim on that couch, and she'd always had feelings for him, that was true, she'd always been attracted to him physically, he was young and strong and free, she felt so warm with him then, and

Tom was a good husband, she loved Tom, she did, but it felt so wonderful being with Jim, who she had always wanted, and who was warm and who was hard and strong and Tom was getting so heavy and he never touched her anymore, sometimes it was like he couldn't stand her, shouldn't it have been the other way around? He was the one who didn't keep in shape, the one who'd let himself go, and she still looked good, didn't she? Wasn't she beautiful? Didn't people look at her on the street and in the grocery store and in the department stores? Men who wanted to be with her and women who wanted to look like her?—and that night with Jim—and she was drunk—but she felt good—Jim had looked at her like she was beautiful, she had seen him looking at her body and on that couch it had felt right and she leaned into him, feeling warm, and he put his arm around her, and she nuzzled in beneath his cheek, he moved and she moved, they moved against each other, and she began to breathe harder, could hear him breathing harder, could feel him breathing, and she closed her eyes, ran her face up his and across to his lips, all without knowing quite what was happening, and she opened her mouth and he his and it was warm and he moved on top of her, lifted her shirt, kissed her chest, gently slid his hand down her pants, she put her hand down his, never opening her eyes for a second, did that for awhile, before it occurred to her that she needed to put a stop to this, that they were going too far together, but she let it go on just a little longer, let herself go on with it because it felt so wonderful, let it go on until the warmth ran into her face and hands, down to her toes and it felt so good, and then she kissed him one last time before the feeling subsided, ran her tongue over and under his, then pulled away. She sat up, pulled her shirt down, and said coldly, No. You can't do this, Jim. You went too far, and she looked at him, his lips parted, strong chin, deep blue eyes and soft lips, childlike, she pulled her shirt down, stood up, walked to the door and opened it. He walked through. Then she closed the door behind him, loudly so that he would know she was disappointed in him, but at the same time she hoped he didn't think she was a tease. She wasn't a tease. She just had to stop sometime and he had gone too far.

Tom came home the next day. She was in the exercise room, running on the treadmill. He walked in and she slowed the machine down to a walking pace and asked him how his trip was. Fine, and he left and soon she heard the shower start. She pressed the up arrow until she was running at a good clip again. Twenty more minutes, then she'd go in and ask him about his trip, but when she finished twenty minutes later, he was in bed, asleep.

Why did Jim do it? Maybe she was his tragic love interest, maybe he had loved her. Maybe this meant a part of her was dying too. She wished she had acted differently after that night, wished she hadn't talked bad about him to Tom, saying things like, I don't know about your brother. There's something not quite right with him. I don't feel comfortable around him. She used to say things like that, and Tom could never have known the real reason she said these things, but she knew he started believing what she said because he'd stopped talking to Jim. A woman can tell about a man, she'd said. A woman knows these things.

And wasn't there a part of her that was relieved that Jim was dead?

Christ Jesus, what a thing to think! What an awful thing to think!

She looked at the crowd, saw Tom with his arm around his mother. They'd all seen her crying. What they must have thought, none of them knowing that she always cried in churches.

Anna stood up and walked outside, dodging people—how could they eat at a time like this?—many of whom wanted to stop her and talk, but she didn't want to talk, she brushed them off, needed to get outside. She walked outside, down the steps, through the grounds of the church, and across the street to a coffee shop. She went in and ordered a nonfat double-tall latté from the boy behind the counter.

Jane and Beth drove Mary to the cemetery, following a long line of cars; Mary in the backseat in her black dress, a veil covering her face, Jane and Beth in the front of Beth's big car. Jane looked back at Mary staring out the window at the houses, children playing, at the trees. Mary began to cry again as they drove through the gates of the cemetery. Oh, sweetheart, Jane said. She reached over the backrest and rubbed her friend's leg.

Husband and mother and son, all gone in just a few years. A tragedy.

Now they sat together beneath a green tarp. Jane had heard it was going to rain, but beyond the tarp, the skies were clear. The priest was speaking, but Jane wasn't listening. She could feel the crowd huddled behind her, heard someone to the side clear his throat. She sat with her arm around Mary. Mary wasn't crying anymore. She was looking down at the grass, at her feet. No, Jane realized, Mary's eyes were closed. It was all so sad.

Jane thought she should, so she tried to put herself in Mary's place, tried to imagine what it would feel like if it was *her* son who had died. She tried to imagine but when she began to feel what it would feel like, when she reached the point in her heart where the feelings began to become real, when she felt her son's mortal absence—and the wind blew across her back and he was dead—she looked up across the casket at her son standing with his wife, both of their heads bowed, eyes closed, hands folded in front of them. She looked at them for awhile in love, then realizing it was inappropriate, insensitive, even selfish, she closed her eyes and tried to listen to the prayer, but she couldn't. She wanted to open her eyes. She tried awhile longer to keep them closed, tried to stay there in the dark with the priest, with the memory of Mary's boy, but she couldn't. She opened her eyes and the afternoon light filled them; she looked up at her son and watched him, his head bowed, while she rubbed Mary's shoulder.

Tom hadn't wanted to go to the site. He would go later, when no one was around and he could be alone. Now he was helping the cleaning woman clean up the reception area. Where do you want this table? he asked her.

You can lean it up against the wall there, she said. She wiped her brow. The heater must be on full blast. It's hot, isn't it?

Yeah, Tom said. He was hot and sweating through his shirt, but it seemed he was always sweating these days.

You know you don't need to do this, the woman said.

It's all right.

It's my job. They pay me to do it.

Really, I don't mind, Tom said. He turned the table on its side and folded the legs underneath.

The woman asked him something he didn't catch.

I'm sorry?

Did you know the man who died? she said again.

Yes, Tom said.

It's very sad.

Yes. It is.

So young, she said.

Tom lifted the table and carried it over to where the woman had directed. She was running a sweeper across the carpet. He walked across the room to where the other table was, swept crumbs off of it with his hand. He looked out the window. Down the hill, beyond some houses, was the Sound. Beyond it, the Olympic Mountain range. It was a clear day. A thin strip of cloud lay high up in the atmosphere; above the clouds, even higher, the sky was clear, white. He turned the table onto its side and folded the legs, picked it up and set it next to the other one. The room was empty now.

Anything else? he said.

No, that's it. I just have to sweep.

Should I take the trash out?

I can do that, she said. The Dumpster's on the way to my car.

You're sure there's nothing else?

I'm sure.

Nothing else I can do?

No. Thank you.

All right, Tom said. He picked his jacket up from the floor and put it on, walked outside. He wondered where Anna was, he hadn't seen her in hours and hadn't thought of her until now. She must have gone home with someone else. Who would she have gone home with? He didn't want to think about that now. Best to rid your mind of everything... Best to think about nothing.

He walked through the grounds, down the steps to the parking lot, towards his car.

There she was. Sleeping. Tom could see her in the front seat, the seat reclined, curled up on her side. He walked down and unlocked his door, got inside.

Anna opened her eyes and stretched. Then she turned and faced forward, brought the seat back to its vertical position, but further forward than she liked. While Tom started the car and pulled out of the parking lot, she fiddled with the handle until she found the right angle. There, she said.

Eric said, I'll miss him.

I know, Marty said. I know. Hey! Somebody pass one of those pitchers this way! and Pete, down at the end of the table, picked up the pitcher in front of him and filled his glass—he was going to pass it down to Marty, but by the time he had filled his glass that guy Rich had passed the one in front of him—and Pete thought, I shouldn't have poured my drink first. But who cared? It was a wake after all and they would all be buying many more pitchers.

The money is the best part, Bill was saying and it took Pete a little while to figure out what he was talking about, but then he remembered: Bill was moving upstairs and out of the warehouse where he was working, moving up into the management part of the company. I couldn't get by on what I was making, Bill said, and I was working there for five years. Angela was about to leave me and find a guy with a salary! Not really, of course, not really, she's not that bad, I talk a lot about her when I drink, but we love each other, don't listen to me when I get like this, Jesus, I don't even remember what I've been talking about all this time, I could've said something real bad and I wouldn't know!

Bill had told himself: Don't talk about Angela tonight. Just don't even mention her at all. At the cemetery, he'd gotten Eric's wife to give Angela a ride home; he'd said to Angela, I won't be late. Just going out with the guys, and Angela had said,

I want you home by eight o'clock. Before the baby goes to bed.

That's pretty early. These guys like to stay out.

Nine o'clock, she said, then she had taken the baby out of his arms and walked away, and he'd been disappointed.

They all took separate cars to the Trolley and Bill had gone straight to the bathroom, combed his hair back in the mirror, straightened his tie, and he thought, You're gonna get drunk tonight. Don't talk about her. You always bitch and moan about her when you drink. Don't even mention her. You'll just look like a fool and nobody will like her.

I really love her, Bill said to Pete. She's the best girl in the world.

You're a lucky man, Pete said.

The best girl in the whole world, Bill said, I mean that, and Pete said,

Yeah.

Rich didn't know why he'd come. He should have gone off somewhere by himself. He'd leave soon. He'd put on his coat and take off. He didn't know these guys, but he had introduced himself to Jim's mother after the service and she had introduced him to this guy Eric and Eric had invited him along and he didn't have anything else to do or anywhere else to go, so he came along. He was tired and worn out. People died all the time. That wasn't a big deal. But Jim was the last guy he would have imagined killing himself. What the hell had been wrong with him? Rich regretted not keeping in touch with Jim. Hell, he almost didn't come to the funeral. He didn't know if it was worth the drive up from Arizona. He didn't know if the type of relationship he'd had with Jim warranted driving all the way up. Had they even been what you'd call friends? They drank together for a time a few years ago. They worked together for the City, partied together, but it was a little strange to drive up to the top of the country for the funeral of a guy you barely knew. Being here at this bar with these guys, strangers, all talking about shit he knew nothing about: people they all knew and had known, places they'd been together—it was occurring to Rich that he hadn't known Jim at all. He hadn't even known that Jim had once been a boxer, a good boxer, a boxer that people had expected might someday go pro. He hadn't known until he'd read the program at the funeral, saw the pictures on the table in the foyer. There were pictures of Jim as a kid, high school graduation pictures, pictures of him with friends, a picture of him holding a baby, the baby dressed in a miniature basketball jersey, and a girl with red hair next to him, smiling.

Rich had wondered if this was the girl he had talked about, the girl he was looking for. Then he'd seen the picture of Jim in his boxing stance:

A tall, wiry dark-haired Irish kid with black shorts and boxing shoes laced high; younger than the Jim he'd known; a pair of red gloves on and a stance that, when you stood in front of the picture, looked like he was going to jump out and pounce on you.

Rich could see the power in him through that stance, and it was something he had noticed before, that Jim, who was very quiet, who always seemed laid-back, who moved slowly and methodically, had, in his reserves, a tremendous physical power. He could tell by the way Jim unscrewed a bottle of beer, the way he shot pool. It was obvious Jim knew how to use his body, knew how to harness his energy.

What the fuck was he talking about, *harness his energy?* What the fuck did that even mean? What was he doing up here?

Rich downed the last of his glass, thought for a second about just leaving, saying goodbye to these four guys who didn't seem to even remember he was there, and just taking off, but he didn't want to get up yet, he wanted to stay and drink some more, so he waved to the bar girl.

She came over. What do you need? she said.

Another pitcher of whatever this is we're drinking.

All right, she said. She smiled, reached over him and took the empty—her hair brushed up against Rich's face, she smelled good—it had been three days since he'd left Tucson and Daisy was waiting for him at home. The waitress walked back towards the bar, short black skirt, tight blouse. He wanted to get laid. The way he felt, all he wanted to do was screw. He'd never been this high up in America before and probably never would be again. Federal Way, Washington. He could probably get away with anything, it occurred to him. Anything in the world. You're never gonna be up here again, Rich. You can do anything, sleep with anyone, be on the freeway in five minutes, headed back home.

He could have been a fucking good boxer for one thing, Eric said.

Yeah, Marty said. I saw him fight. He could be a monster in the ring, but he was always good to his friends.

Yeah.

Marty said, He could be a monster if he wanted to but you knew nothing was going to happen to you. He wasn't going to let anything happen to his friends. He loved his friends. He loved his friends more than anything.

Let me ask you something, Eric said. He lowered his head and Marty drew closer. Did he ever say anything to you? Did he ever say anything? Was he depressed? Was he fucked-up? Was he using again? Was there something I didn't know? and Eric really wanted to know, he needed to know because it had been eating him up the past four days.

When he heard about it, at first he hadn't believed—he'd gotten the call from Jim's brother, and it had been a short call and Eric hadn't believed it. A short call and Eric hung up, shaking his head—What the hell was that all about? What's going on? Jamie! he'd shouted. Jamie!

What? his wife had shouted back. I'm watching TV!

He walked into the living room, light-headed. I just got this call from Tom. He said Jimmy shot himself.

What are you talking about? she said. No, he didn't. I saw him two days ago.

Oh God fuck wait, Eric said. Wait, wait. What the fuck? he said, and then he went downstairs into the laundry room and locked the door, Jamie calling after him:

I'm calling their mom! Tell her her asshole kids should not be making prank calls like this! It's fucking immature!

and Eric sat down on the toilet and was going to cry, but he didn't cry because he was too confused. *What the hell is this?* *Wait. What the hell is this, man? Do you know?* Who he was talking to, he had no idea; his head hurt, his brain, he felt, was trying to break out of his skull and float upstairs through the ceiling, where he could hear Jamie yelling:

I'm calling her! She needs to tell those brats that some things aren't funny!

but Eric knew it was true, he knew it was true that Jimmy was dead, knew it was true because—and this didn't make sense at all, did it?—because he couldn't feel Jimmy on the earth anymore.

What?

I said he didn't kill himself, Marty said. It wasn't suicide. I know it. Call it a hunch or whatever, but I know what happened and it makes sense if you knew Jim. He liked to gamble, right? You know that. You remember.

Eric said, Yeah, I remember.

Well, that's the thing, Marty said. It wasn't suicide, man. My theory is he was playing Russian roulette and he lost.

Russian roulette?

Yeah, Marty said, and you know what that means.

What?

That means somebody was with him when he died. Somebody was there. Somebody saw him blow his brains out, then that *somebody* picked up the fucking money and walked out the door. Maybe even somebody who was at the funeral. Hey, Marty whispered, what about this guy?

Eric looked at Rich, who was turned around in his seat, talking to the waitress. She was crouching down next to him, smiling; she smoothed her hair back.

What do people do around here for fun? Rich said.

I don't know, she said. Not much. I guess you're doing it.

I like your bracelet.

Thanks.

Your boyfriend give you that bracelet?

I don't have a boyfriend.

That's too bad.

What are you guys all dressed up for?

Funeral, Rich said.

Oh, the waitress said. She looked into Rich's eyes. Who was it?

A friend of ours.

He was young?

Twenty-six.

That's awful. She put her hand on Rich's leg. I'm sorry. You were close?

Yes.

I had a friend who died, she said. Car accident. That was years ago. I'm still not over it.

I guess some things you never get over.

Yeah.

Eric was explaining to Marty that he seriously doubted it was Russian roulette—You're drunk—and if it *had* been Russian roulette, this guy Rich didn't have anything to do with it. Eric told Marty how Rich had known Jim when Jim was down in Arizona, how Tom had called him, and he'd driven up.

Well, anyway, Marty said. He downed his beer and poured himself another one. Maybe he owed somebody money and they came to collect, he said. Some big-shot gambler or something. He shook his head, staring down at the table. Shit, I don't know...

Eric leaned back in his chair. He looked up at the ceiling. It was dark in the bar, but there were distinct water stains on the ceiling above him, the edges curving and curling in strange patterns. Well, it was *probably* water. What else could it be? In places the tiles were rotted through and falling apart, drooping down above the people in the bar. There was one right above Bill. It was going to fall. It was strange that in all the nights in all the years Eric had been here, he'd never noticed them. He would have hated to see the place in the light. He said: You ever known Jim to be depressed?

No, Marty said.

You ever know Jim to want to kill himself?

No.

I just don't know why he did it, Eric said.

Fuck if I know, the asshole, Marty said. He downed his glass again and poured another. Lost his fucking mind, he said. That girl of his taking off might of had something to do with it. What was her name?

Julie, Eric said.

Yeah. Julie. I wonder what happened to her.

Bill was drinking faster, watching this guy he didn't know put the moves on the bar girl. He thought: Angela, someday, I'm gonna snap. You're gonna call me another name, you're gonna yell and shriek about how I'm worthless, about how no matter what I do, I'm stupid, I'm stupid and an idiot, and I'm no good and I'm poor and stupid, and I don't know anything, and people see me and they know I'm dumb, I'm stupid, I'm not gonna do anything with my life—you're gonna say that one too many times, that WORD, that fucking word I hate. *STUPID*. Just one more time. Say it. I dare you. Say it one more time. *STUPID*. Say it one more fucking time. I *STUPID* dare you. Just one more time. One more *STUPID* time.

I'm telling you, Pete said. Hey, Bill. Hey Bill!

What? Bill said.

Am I boring you? Pete said.

Not really, Bill said.

Well, let me know if I'm boring you.

Bill said, I gotta take a piss. He stood up, still staring at the waitress—he was drunk—he never drank this much anymore, had to put his hands on the table to keep from tipping over—Jesus, she had her hand on the guy's leg—Bill walked over to her, looked down, his groin by her face, staggering, right in her fucking face. He said, Where's the bathroom? and she took her hand off the guy's leg, and stood up quickly.

Back there, she said, pointing. Through that door. Haven't you been here before? she said.

Nope, Bill said. I've never been here before. Never. He turned and under his breath he said, Stupid bitch.

Excuse me? What was that? she said.

But Bill was already walking towards the bathroom.

Did you hear what he just said to me! she said.

Hey, I don't even know him, Rich said.

Pete said, What did he say?

He called me a stupid bitch!

Bill said that?

Bill said what? Eric said.

He called the waitress a stupid bitch.

Bill didn't say that, Marty said.

The hell he didn't! the waitress said.

Bill wouldn't say something like that. I know Bill and Bill wouldn't say something like that. You must have misunderstood.

Look asshole, I heard *exactly* what he said!

Now who's calling names?

Another pitcher, please, Eric said.

The waitress stormed away, and Pete and Marty and Eric laughed, but Rich just stared at them, couldn't say anything because he didn't know them, but if one of his buddies back home would have messed up something like that—and he was doing good with her, he could have gotten somewhere with her, was about to ask her what time she got off, tell her he didn't have a place to stay for the night, maybe she had an idea?—if his buddies back home would have messed it up for him like that he would have beaten the shit out of them, he'd have taken them outside and boxed their fucking heads in, no matter what, no matter what day it was!

He squeezed the glass in his hand, hoping it would break and cut into him. It didn't break. He was sorry.

But there was death. And all he could think of—

All he wanted to do was get laid.

She needs some Valium, Jane said. I have some in my purse. I keep it for occasions like this.

Good, Beth said. I could use one myself. They were in the upstairs hallway, outside Mary's bedroom. They could hear Mary crying:

—*My baby! My baby!*

The best thing in a time like this is sleep, Beth said. How many are you going to give her?

I don't know. I never use them. One?

—*My baby! My baby!*

One doesn't sound like enough.

What do you think? Two? Jane said.

—*Ohhhhhhh...*

Maybe four or five. Give her a lot. We want her to fall asleep. Do you have that many?

Jane looked in her purse. Where are they? Here they are. She opened the vial, shook it. I've got four.

I wish you had more. I wouldn't mind one myself.

Me too.

Do you think two would be enough for her?

Maybe. I don't know. Do you think?

I don't know.

I don't know either.

We should probably give her at least three, Beth said.

Split one?

Sure.

They went downstairs and into Mary's kitchen. Beth found a glass and filled it with tapwater, while Jane took a carving knife out of a drawer and pulled the cutting board out from its place above the silverware drawer.

She's quiet now, Beth said.

Jane set a small pill on the cutting board and with the knife attempted to cut the pill in half, pressed down hard—These pills are hard as rocks!—put her weight into it and the knife came down hard, she felt, heard, half of the pill whizz by her ear. Oh! Where'd it go? Beth picked up her half from the cutting board and Jane walked a few steps and got on her knees, put her left cheek against the linoleum, closing her right eye, and looked for a bump on the floor's horizon, the pill. She couldn't see it, so she crawled around with her face against the floor, looking.

Do you see it? Beth said.

No, said Jane, crawling. She remembered Mary's son and her own son, years ago, so long ago, but didn't it seem like just a day or a week or a month? Mary would come over to Jane's house during the week or she would come here to Mary's and they would drink tea and talk and read from Dr Spock; they were so young then, just starting out, two young girls who loved their children more than their own lives, confessing that they would trade their husbands in for another child and laughing, saying, Husbands are like used cars, and laughing more while their babies crawled around beneath their feet, and then their babies grew up and there'd been a time when Jane didn't think Eric was going to make it, a time when he was in so much pain and she worried he might do something drastic because the situation was drastic, and the doctors couldn't help and God didn't help no matter how much she prayed, and she would sit up all night waiting for him, worrying herself sick, worrying about where he was, who he was with, what they were doing. Well, he made it, didn't he? He made it. But Jim didn't make it. Mary's son Jim didn't make it. And now he'd never have the chance to—

There it is. It was on the carpet, below the doorway where the living room met the kitchen. There it is.

Jane got up, walked over and picked up the half-pill and put it on her tongue. She swallowed it down dry. Beth took a sip from Mary's glass and swallowed hers. Then the two women walked through the living room, Beth holding the glass, Jane holding the vial, up the stairs and into the bedroom.

Mary was curled up on her side in her black dress, her back to them, the veil beside her.

Mary, Beth said.

Mary, we have something for you. It'll make you feel better, sweetheart.

When Bill came back from the bathroom, he picked up his jacket off the back of his chair and said to Pete, I'll be right back. I'm going out to my car for a second. Then he had walked outside into dusk. In the dark of the bar it had felt like the middle of the night, but the clock on the bank across the street said seven o'clock. It was almost winter and the sun was setting earlier. Only seven o'clock. He'd told Angela he would be home by nine. He had two hours. What could he do in that time? He got in his car and pulled out of the parking lot, drove north up Pac-Highway, away from the bar, away from his apartment. What was he going to do? Where was he going to go? It was Friday and he couldn't think of a thing. But one thing was for certain, he wasn't going back to the Trolley. That only depressed him worse. He didn't like those guys. Eric was all right, but the rest of them... He hated Marty and always had and Pete was just too boring to put into words. It wasn't like when they were kids. Back then they all knew where they were coming from. They were young and dumb and they understood each other. Now, he had to admit he didn't really know any of them anymore and he didn't care to. He missed Jim. Jim was the only one he'd never stopped caring for. He missed Jim terribly. Jim was the one he could talk to, the only one he felt he could tell the truth to; the truth about his job and how he was lowman, how he'd been there for seven years and how everyone he'd started with—and many of those who'd started after him—had moved up in the company a long time ago. Hell, even this new promotion wasn't really a promotion. He was moving upstairs, sure, but he was going to be in charge of inventory, a job that no one wanted, a job that had been offered to almost everyone before him and they had all turned it down. He was going to hate it. He would be off the floor, he would have his own desk and cubicle when he started on Monday, but he was only making a few cents more an hour and it was the worst job in the entire place. The only reason he'd taken the position was because Angela didn't know what sort of job it was, he took it because he thought she would be proud of him, she would think that he was moving up. If Jim was here Bill could tell him all about it. He would call Jim up and say, unafraid of what he sounded like because Jim never cared about shit like that—Hell, he had *cried* in front of Jim—he would call Jim up and say, Man, this job is a piece of shit. I only got it because no one else wanted it, and Jim would say, Don't worry about it. You'll do a good job and then they'll move you higher. And anyways you're off the floor. You get to wear a suit and tie. What are you talking about it's not a promotion? Of course it's a promotion! You moved up! You're upstairs now! Nobody wanted it because they were all too scared they'd fuck it up! Those fuckers couldn't handle the responsibility! You're perfect for the job! What are you moaning about? and Bill would say, Yeah, I guess you're right. I guess you got a point. I don't know what I was thinking, and Jim would say, Of course you don't know what you're thinking. Besides, it could be worse.

You could be a fucking trashboy like me, and they would laugh. Bill knew Jim would say these things, he knew he would feel better if Jim was around, he knew the words Jim would say, but in his head they meant nothing without the right voice behind them.

Why did things always change for the worse? Did it ever get better for anyone? Besides people who win the lottery? What if he fucked up in his new job? What if he didn't do it right? Then what? Would they move him back downstairs? Or would they just tell him to take a hike? He wasn't lazy, he just wasn't that good at things. There wasn't anything he was good at or had ever been good at. What will Angela say if they fire him? Damn. He shouldn't have taken the job. He should have just stayed downstairs and kept his mouth shut.

She had loved him. Now he didn't think she loved him at all. She was disappointed in him, thought he wasn't anything special, and he wasn't. He was sorry he disappointed her. He wanted to be something special, do something extraordinary. Maybe if he kept driving it would come to him. But driving up this street, this street that never changed, this street that had always been the same since he could remember, the same gas stations, the same convenience stores and fast food joints, the same muffler shops, porno stores, the old drive-in, the same dark shapes of strangers waiting for busses and for lights to change, driving up this ugly street was like walking against a conveyor belt, not getting anywhere, but afraid to stop because the moment you stopped it took you further back than you'd been when you started. So he kept on going.

They'd planned on going out, they'd planned on making a day of it, going to the beach, maybe, driving along the water, maybe window shopping in Seattle. But when Robert saw Ruth come out of the shower, her short hair slicked to her head, her face pink and flushed from the hot water, her skin shining, when he saw her come out of the shower, that yellow towel wrapped around her, over her breasts, under her arms, he hadn't wanted to do anything but take her to bed. So they'd gotten in bed, they made love, they fell asleep holding each other, and later she'd woken him up with her mouth on his, kissing him softly, and they'd made love again, then fell asleep again, and now they were awake again. Robert felt soft and warm all over. He couldn't remember the last time they'd spent a day like this. Aside from the pain in his head and neck and back, and aside from his hands, he felt good, and when they'd been having sex he hadn't had any pain at all, and aside from the pain now, he felt good. But then he thought again of Pierce. Should he have gone to the funeral? He didn't know. He didn't know Pierce, had never known him outside the ring.

But there'd been a time, hadn't there? A time when they had talked. He tried to remember. A conversation. A few days after the second fight, the fight when Pierce wouldn't go down and Robert called the ref to put a stop to it. Where had they run into each other?

At the Trolley. And he saw the kid's face. The left side, purple and yellow, a blurry line of bruises from his swollen nose to his chin. A cut below his left eye was taped and the white part of the eye was wet and red from a burst blood vessel. Robert remembered what the kid had looked like; he saw the image in his mind, he could recall that. But what did they talk about? He couldn't remember. It seemed now, somehow very important.

Hello? Ruth said. Anyone home?

Yeah?

I asked you what you're thinking about. Her head was on his chest and he put his hand on the top of her head and moved it gently down the side of her face.

Nothing, he said.

Nothing? You must be thinking about *something.*

Just laying here.

Your head hurt?

Yeah.

My baby. She kissed his chest. My baby, she said. My big, strong old man.

Robert laughed for her.

She said, We need to do this more often.

Yeah.

Wouldn't it be wonderful if we could spend every day like this?

Yeah.

We used to stay in bed all day, remember?

Yeah, Robert said, and he did.

I wish you were around more, she said. It's like I never see you anymore. You know? I don't know if I like your new boss, she said. He works you too hard. He's too young, anyway. A kid like that shouldn't be telling you what to do. You know ten times what he does.

That's the way it goes sometimes.

Ruth said, Maybe I could get a part-time job.

No.

I could work a few hours here and there, just to take care of the computer payments and things.

No job.

You wouldn't have to work so much, she said. Besides, I think I might like it. Something to get me out of the house while Amy's at school. That girl loves her computer, Ruth said. She's quick with stuff like that. She was showing me email this morning.

She's quick, Robert said.

She doesn't get it from me, that's for sure.

Ruth rolled over onto her back. Robert heard her sigh. She said,

I really should have gone to church today.

Yeah?

I told them I'd help set up for the wedding tomorrow. You remember the wedding? I told you about it last week. I asked you to get the day off and you couldn't.

Right.

I'm sure they managed without me.

Robert didn't say anything.

One of these days you're going to come back, Ruth said.

Back where?

To church. To *God*. You're going to come back someday.

Keep praying, he said.

I will, she said. I'll keep praying. I'm *always* praying. Then they lay for a time without saying anything. Robert closed his eyes. There was something he was forgetting, but he didn't know what.

He heard Ruth say, Let's get up. I'll make something to eat,

and he opened his eyes when he felt her move from the bed. She was scooting to the bathroom, an open hand covering her rear end. She turned her head and looked back at him, smiling, as she went through the door.

Tom called his mother's house. She's asleep, Beth said. She'll be out for the rest of the night. You just stay home and take care of your wife. Come by tomorrow, Tom. The family will all be here then. We'll stay with her tonight.

Bill turned off Pac-Highway, drove up 200th, got into the turn lane, sped through a yellow, swung right, north, merged onto the freeway...

It was Tom, Beth said. She sat back down at the kitchen table. Picked up the deck and started shuffling. I told him she'll be out for the rest of the night. I said we'd stay with her tonight.

What this time? Jane said.

Beth thought about it.

Five card draw?

Wild?

Beth thought about it. What was lucky? How about seven? Seven was always lucky. Sevens wild, she said.

You shuffle, Jane said. I need to make a call. She got up and dialed her son's house. Jamie answered. Jane loved Jamie. How fortunate her son was to have a companion like her.

Jamie said Eric was out with the boys.

I'll try back later then, Jane said. I love you both so much, you know.

I know, Jane. We love you too.

I just wanted to tell you again.

We know, Jane. Thank you. It's been a hard day, hasn't it.

I don't want you to forget.

We won't forget. How's Mary?

She's fine. Sleeping now.

And how are you? Jamie said.

Fine, dear. I'll let you go now. Give Eric my love when he gets home.

Jamie said, I will.

Rich said: Hey, baby, it's me. I'll probably leave here in the morning. I thought you'd be home. You're probably asleep. Are you there? Hello? Hello? Hello-hello? Yes? No? All right. Maybe you're out. You there? Guess not. Well. That's about it. I'll leave here tomorrow. I should be back Sunday. See you then, he said. Bye. Good night.

Then he hung up the phone, pulled down on the change

release—nothing— walked out of the back room, past a couple guys in flannel playing pool, back to the table. I'd better get going, he said, but no one heard him. They were arguing over a random bit of local sports trivia: who had hit the winning shot in some game some year.

Rich grabbed his jacket, looked at the bar—the waitress gone—and walked out. Until the door closed behind him, he could hear their shouts:

Sikma!

No, not Sikma! Sikma was at Milwaukee then!

I'm telling you, Sikma!

It wasn't Sikma!

Then who was it?

How the hell should I know?

The readout said Anna had run for sixty-eight minutes straight, had burned eight hundred eighty-four calories. An eight-minute mile. Thirteen calories a minute. She would keep going. She'd try for a personal best.

When the baby had finally fallen asleep—and weren't babies supposed to sleep all day long? This one was always wide awake. Someday when he was grown she would tell him stories about what a fussy baby he'd been—Angela set him down in his crib and walked around the apartment, finally able to finish her dusting. She wouldn't vacuum. It would wake him. She'd wait to vacuum when he was awake. In the meantime, there was still so much to do. The laundry needed doing—Bill was going to need his new shirts pressed now that he was moving upstairs in the company, she would have to iron out all the creases, he couldn't show up looking like he'd just taken them out of the package. There was laundry to do and dishes in the sink. When was she going to have a dishwasher? When was she going to have a house of her own? She wanted two stories, a large master bedroom with an adjoining bathroom, shower and bath, large bay windows, a view of something, a balcony overlooking some woods, maybe, or a view of Mount Rainier. Something with a view of the Sound would be perfect, but she knew that wasn't going to happen. With what Bill made, she couldn't afford something like that. Housing prices in Federal Way were through the roof these days. Her parents had bought their house in the mid-seventies for twenty thousand dollars. Now it was worth more than two hundred. How are you supposed to get anywhere these days? You probably couldn't get a *trailer* for less than eighty grand! That would be a laugh! Her parents would *love that*, her living in a trailer. As it was, she and Bill could barely afford the rent for *this* dump! She had quit her job at the doctor's office to have the baby. She'd have to go back before long. Bills were adding up. Credit card companies calling. She wanted to stay home and take care of the baby. She wanted a man who could support her. Bill couldn't support her. Whose fault was that? Bill's? If he would have been more motivated, if he would have gone to business school like he'd told her so long ago. I want to go into business for myself, he'd said. Be my own boss. But that was just a pipe dream, wasn't it? Bill didn't have that kind of mind. He'd make an *awful* businessman. Forget it.

Maybe it was America's fault. It was too hard to get anywhere in this stupid country today.

What was she going to do with the baby when she went back to work? Daycare was too expensive. Maybe her mother would take care of him. Then she'd really hear it:

A mother shouldn't work! A mother shouldn't pass her children off to relatives! Babies need their mothers and besides it's your responsibility! You can't just dish off your problems to family! I was home for all of you! I didn't miss a second of it! It was my responsibility! It was my job!

Well, that was a different time! It's different now!

She would never again ask her parents for money, never ask for their help, never again, she wondered how much money Bill was spending at the bar and thinking about it made her angry. When's the last time *I* went out with *my* friends? When's the last time *I* bought myself something! And he was probably showing off—buying the first pitcher, keeping them coming, letting those stupid friends of his get by without paying when it was their turn! We don't have that kind of money! Why wasn't he responsible! Always showing off! Always trying to keep the stupid party going! *Look at me! I'm Bill! Look at me!* Damnit William! Take a look in the mirror! Take a look in the *stupid* mirror!

She was in the living room now, bent over, furiously wiping down the wooden frame of the coffee table and she—she knew he was spending all their money!—slammed the dust spray canister down on the glass and cracked it. The crack ran from one end to the other, but she didn't care. Bill had brought it home from the Salvation Army, what a prize! She tossed the rag on the ground and didn't pick it up, fell into the couch, grabbed the remote, and stabbed the air with it until the stupid TV came on.

The chandelier was shaking. Tom wiped pizza grease off his fingers with a cloth napkin and turned the volume up on the TV. He stretched out on the couch. He loosened his tie and undid the buckle on his belt.

Jimmy.

Why had he done it? Why hadn't he come to him if he had a problem? They were brothers. Maybe they didn't talk anymore, but they were still brothers. There wasn't a fight or an argu-

ment or a woman in the world that could change that. What
did you have if you didn't have family?

Stay away from my wife, Tom had said. He'd gone over to
Jimmy's boarding house. Jimmy was living in one small room,
had been for a few months since coming back from Arizona.
He hadn't found his girlfriend. He hadn't found his kid. He
wasn't fighting anymore. He hadn't fought in a long time. Tom
hated to see Jimmy at the boarding house, hated seeing the way
Jimmy lived. Jimmy didn't have anything. Not a TV or a stereo,
not even a couch. He had a tiny refrigerator and a hot plate.
There was a scummy old fishtank on the floor with nothing
in it. No water, no fish. Just some rocks on the bottom and a
plastic diver without legs. Tom would have to go someday and
retrieve these things. Jimmy slept in a sleeping bag on the floor,
read books, listened to the radio. He was working for the sani-
tation department. It had been embarrassing to Tom, and he
knew he hadn't been a good brother to Jimmy. He should have
gotten him a job at his office. He should have offered him a
place to stay. Tom and Anna had more rooms than they knew
what to do with. But the night he told Jimmy to stay away from
his wife, he wasn't thinking of any of this, he was not thinking
that he had been a bad brother to Jimmy. His mom had said,

You need to talk to your brother about your wife.

Why? Tom had said.

I'm not going to get into it, she said. I'm your boys' mother. I
just think you should have a talk with him about Anna.

Why should I talk to him about Anna?

All I'm saying...

Why should I talk to him about Anna, Mom?

Just talk to him.

Why?

They were over here the other night when you were on your
fishing trip.

So? Tom said.

I'm just saying, talk to him.

Why should I talk to him?

They were drinking. You know how people get when they drink.

How do they get?

You know how they get.

No. I don't. How did they get?

It's nothing. They looked like they were getting close is all.

Tom drove straight over. He walked up the stairs to Jimmy's room. Jimmy opened the door. Tommy, he said, smiling.

Stay away from my wife, Tom said.

What?

You heard me.

What are you talking about?

Stay away from her, Tom said. I see the way you look at her. I got eyes.

You don't know what you're talking about.

You should hear the way she talks about you. She doesn't want you. You're a hoodlum. You're a loser. She thinks you're a loser. She tells me that. You think she doesn't know that? We all know what you are. Anna knows it. Mom knows it. We all know it.

Well, thanks for stopping by.

You take her home?

What?

Did you take her home from Mom's house?

Yeah I took her home. She was drunk. You want me to let her crash her car? She was loaded.

So you felt it was your duty to take her home and put her to bed.

Yeah, Jimmy said. I did. She could've wrecked that brand new car of yours. Then you would've been *real* mad.

I'll tell you one last time. Stay away from her.

You don't know what you're talking about, Jimmy said. And that wife of yours is not as innocent as you think.

What's that supposed to mean?

Nothing. Bye. Jimmy made a move to close the door but Tom stuck his foot in front of it.

What's that supposed to mean!

Nothing. Bye.

Tom leaned into him, whispered, You think I can't take you you little piece of shit?

I think you're a bit out of shape.

You think I can't box your ears? Remember I broke your arm? You think I can't do that again?

Why don't you go eat a sandwich and think it over—

—Tom put his hand around Jimmy's throat but in one swift motion Jimmy knocked the hand away with his right, pushed Tom back with his left; it happened quickly and in an instant Tom's heart was racing, he couldn't breathe right—*Rage* and he wanted to kill the motherfucker; he wanted to tear out his eyes, break his arms, pull off his goddamn legs, rip his fucking dick off. But instead, he only stepped further back from the door, wiped the sweat off his forehead.

He said, You're nothing, you little fuck. You'll always be nothing. You're never gonna be anything. Then he walked away, down the hall, and as Jimmy was shutting the door, Tom turned back, yelled:

Remember when you started you thought you were gonna be champ? You remember you were gonna be champ? You remember? You remember telling me you were gonna be champion of the world? Well you weren't even champion of Federal Way!

When he got home that night, Tom had walked upstairs. The door to the exercise room was open, he peeked in, he saw his wife in profile, running. She was wearing her spandex running outfit, listening to music on her headphones. She was beautiful, had a long, beautiful stride; her ponytail swung back and forth as she ran, she had the sort of body, was a girl that any man would die for. Anna.

And he could hear her now upstairs running. Each time her foot came down, the chandelier above him shook.

That had been only two years ago, that incident at Jimmy's house. They never talked again and now they never would. Tom hadn't regretted confronting Jimmy. He'd told himself it had been the right thing to do. He had defended his honor and the honor of his wife. But now that Jimmy wasn't around anymore, Tom felt he would give anything in the world to talk once more, as brothers.

Bill was far north of the city, out in farm country. The sun was down now, below the horizon, up someplace over the other side of the world. Here, the stars were out. And the wind, rushing around his head, filling the car... He wasn't going to get home by nine. No way. He was too far away now. He laughed. Oh, well. If she didn't like it...

Ninety-eight minutes and Anna was still strong. It was exhilarating. She couldn't feel anything, she was in a zone, no longer needed determination to keep going—she kept going because now she was in the zone, she ran independently of her mind, independently of her will, she was hypnotized, could feel herself inching towards a state of equilibrium where everything: mind body everything was in tune, she'd never been there, she'd almost been there, had felt herself lightening once and knew the equilibrium would be akin to transcendence, no one would understand this who wasn't a runnerandTomwanted-ababy but she didn't want to ruin her body, didn't want floppy breasts and varicose veins, stretch marks, didn't want to get fat, knew she'd never breastfeed, your nipples turn into faucets and it's so gross, childbirth, it's *unnatural* doing that to your body and it was her fault that Tom hadn't talked to his brother, how horrible it must feel to Tom, how he must hate her now, and what if the situation were reversed, what if she'd had an argument with her sister Katy and they didn't speak for two years and what if Katy died without there ever having been resolution, how awful she would feel, and Anna put herself in that mindset, she was able to convince herself for a moment that the situation was reversed, that she hadn't spoken to Katy in two years and that Katy had killed herself, it was true for a moment, and she kept running, and understood, and in that moment something like a pit opened up inside her and she fell into it and knew that she would never be able to find her way out because time had stopped for Katy, and they would never be together again, they would never be able to forgive, and time went on for her, Anna, as it went on for Tom, and it had stopped for Jim and there was no changing things, there was no changing anything, no going back, then the tape was over and Anna could hear the whirring of the treadmill and the thump thump thump of her stride, could hear herself breathing, she knew Katy was down in Oregon with her husband and childrenTomhatesyou, she thought, you won't have his babyyou talked so much bad about his brother and didn't want them to see each other because of fear and shame and don't you remember what you told him at the church before the priest, that you would always be true to him, that you would never put another before him, and you cried? but you did put someone before him didn't you? yes, said always love and cherish and never put anyone before but there is no always is there? no, because always doesn't exist in life does it? no, show me if you can find it, I can't, butneverisreal yes never is real never is everywhere I see it everywhere and we are filled with it we who are living are filled with never and death and dread and always is nowhere but in death, yes always is dead, and Jim and Christ is dead, she felt a bit lightheaded but resolved to keep going—no, not resolve, she didn't need resolve to keep going, all she needed was to follow her feet, lose herself, forget, but she was weakandtired had come out of the zone and her knees were killingher and her head was getting lighter and exhausted and not enough oxygen and looked down at the readout and blinked her eyes because the numbers were blurry and sweat running into her eyes and wiped her eyes but it didn't help, she kept running, her body straight, arms loose, headback headback headback: she could make it further, if she could find that zone, again

There was one right there, on the other side of the street, next to that telephone booth. Rich would have to make a U-turn, not here, there was a barrier in the middle of the highway. An intersection up ahead, he kept driving, got in the left turn lane, stopped abruptly as the light went red. He looked in his rearview mirror. There she was. He said,

Don't stop, Don't stop, Don't stop,

to each car that passed by her. She was pacing up and down the sidewalk, lit up by a red neon Crestview Motel sign. It was dark out and when she stepped out from under the sign, her shape seemed to disappear. Now he couldn't see her this far down the street but when he'd passed he saw she was good-looking, short skirt, thin legs, blonde hair down just past her ears and a long-sleeve shirt. She must be cold. It's cold out tonight.

Someone honked and Rich looked up, saw the light had turned, he stepped on the gas, pulled a U-turn in the middle of the intersection and drove back, saying

Don't stop, Don't stop, Don't stop

to the cars ahead of him, but none of them stopped, they all drove past her. Rich slowed, pulled over a few yards away. He turned his head and she sauntered over to him. His heart was beating fast. He cleared his throat, tried to stay calm. This wasn't his kind of thing. He didn't do this, but who cared? He was in Washington, sixteen hundred miles, twenty-four hours, from home, practically in another country, and Daisy would never find out. Oh, he needed it. He pressed down on his groin with his forearm. The girl opened the door, leaned in, low-cut shirt, a red tear-shaped pendant swinging between her breasts.

Hi, she said.

Hi.

Can I get in?

Yeah, Rich said. She got in, crossed her legs. Nylons underneath her skirt.

Let's go, she said. Turn on that street. And Rich drove, took a right onto the street she pointed to. A block from the highway, the street was dark. Pull over here, she said.

What?

Stop here, she said, and he did, he pulled onto the soft shoulder. Evergreens towered over them.

I thought we could go back to my motel, Rich said.

We can, she said. First we make arrangements. What is it you want?

Rich cleared his throat. He looked at her face. She was leaning towards him, staring into his eyes, controlled. He felt nervous and uncontrolled, which made his breathing terse, his heart race, his forehead sweat. She reached across him and put her hand on the wheel, stroked it with her fingers.

Well? she said.

Everything, Rich said.

Everything? she said. Well, I can do everything. I'd like to do that for you.

And he took his eyes off of her because in his peripheral he saw movement, a shape, he looked ahead, saw headlights where a car was turning onto his road from a side street and headed towards him.

Everything, she said, and Rich kept his eyes on the car and—couldn't be sure because it was dark but—*Oh, no*—blue and red lights and the car sped up, rushed up towards him, came to a quick angled halt in front of his bumper, half on the road, half off—*Oh, no*—he looked in the rearview, another car had pulled out from the highway and was rushing towards his rear, lights spinning, seemed to slide up to him, stopped, Rich looked forward again—two cops leaping from the car—turned his head—behind him the same thing—looked at the girl but she was no longer looking at him. She was fiddling with the key in the ignition, her bracelets jingling. She turned the car off, jiggled the key, her tongue over her bottom lip, concentrating, she found the latch mechanism on the steering column, pressed it, and pulled the key free.

Bill had forgotten about the border.

There was a loud and heavy thud from above and the crystal pendants of the chandelier crashed against one another, violently. Tom opened his eyes. He sat up. Then he jumped up, ran up the stairs, stumbling, breathing hard, down the hall, into the exercise room. Anna was lying on her back next to the treadmill, treadmill whirring. Blood on her face. Her eyes were open, staring up at the ceiling. Tom knelt over her. Anna! he said, but she didn't respond. Anna! Hey! Anna! What happened! Blood from her nose, swollen and purple, he lifted her head to keep the blood from running down into her throat, he'd seen them do it to Jimmy in the ring. She, still looking up towards the ceiling with an empty gaze. Her forehead wet. Tom put his hand on her burning forehead. Anna! But she didn't respond.

Goddamn treadmill; he couldn't handle the noise, couldn't think straight. Call 911? He set her head down, gently, then picked it up again, because he didn't know if he should leave her. Anna! Annalise! Wake up! Annalise! It's Tom! Wake up!

He set her head down gently again and rolled her onto her side. Blood ran onto the carpet. He got up and ran into the bedroom, picked up the phone. Dialed. Somebody get down here right away! There's been an accident! Now, right now! *Can't wait!* Then back into the exercise room, knelt down, but that god-damn machine, stood again and slammed his fists against the control panel, but the fucking thing wouldn't go off, kept slam-ming, kept punching, hitting, brought his elbow up high, then brought it down, hard, control panel, still it kept going, he did this twice, then three times, nothing, noticed a red string attached to a plastic key, pulled it and finally the belt stopped.

He got down next to Anna, fallen, bleeding from her nose, probably broken, took her head, put it in his lap, stroked her wet hair, said, OK relax now, love. Relax. You're gonna be OK. They're coming to help you. They're coming. They're coming to help you now.

I'm tired, Beth said. Jane had taken all of her pennies. Jane was a much better card player than she. It had been a long day.

I am too, Jane said. I should call Paul. Tell him I'm going to sleep here tonight.

I'll stay too.

No, you should go. She doesn't need both of us. She'll be fine. She'll sleep till the morning. Maybe come back in the morning. We'll make her breakfast, comb her hair.

Such a sorrow, Beth said.

A tragedy.

It would be easier for her if Dick were still alive.

He was always so wonderful to her.

Not like her first husband, Beth said.

Yes, Jane said. And God knows where he is now.

He could be alive or dead and we wouldn't know.

No, we wouldn't, Jane said.

And of course there's a baby out there somewhere.

Yes.

The two women sat, looking down at the pennies on the table. Beth looked at Jane and said,

What would you do if your boy did what Mary's did?

Jane said, I don't think we should talk about that. We shouldn't talk about that. I just thank the Lord he's doing fine.

Of course.

Beth put the cards back in the box and put the box back in her purse.

Hold on a minute, Jane said, and she flattened the pile of pennies in front of her and pushed them together, flat to the table. She split them in half with the side of her hand and pushed half over to her friend. Here, Jane said.

No, Beth said. You won them fair and square. They're yours. I'm not a sore loser.

Take them, Jane said.

No, I really couldn't.

Please, Jane said. Take them. It doesn't seem right. I want to call it even.

Beth understood. OK. She took her coin purse out, opened it, and slid the pennies off the table into the purse. A few fell onto the floor, but she didn't have the heart to pick them up. I'll see you tomorrow, Beth said, and she stood and walked to the door, which Jane opened for her. Then she walked down the walk, got into her car and drove home, hurried home.

Jane went upstairs and looked in on Mary, at her huddled shape in the dark.

Mary? she said. Mary? Are you awake?

No answer. So Jane went down into the kitchen and called her husband. It rang five times before he answered. Hi Paul, she said.

Hey. Where are you?

I'm at Mary's. I'm going to stay with her tonight.

OK.

You sound sleepy. Were you asleep?

Fell asleep in front of the TV, Paul said. What time is it?

Almost ten.

Work tomorrow.

Tomorrow's Saturday, Jane said.

That's right. He yawned.

Let's go somewhere tomorrow, Jane said, looking down at the linoleum floor. For a drive, maybe. Beth is going to come back in the morning and take care of Mary and her family will all be here and maybe you and I can spend some time together.

OK, Paul said.

Jane pressed the phone to her cheek. She put her hand to her forehead. She began to cry.

Are you crying? Paul said. Honey, what's the matter? What is it? Why are you crying?

I don't know. Nothing. I'm fine. It's been a long day.

What's the matter, baby?

It's just so sad, Paul. It's just all so sad.

What's so sad?

Everything.

Why don't I come over there, Paul said.

No, you don't need to do that, Jane said. I'll be fine.

I'm coming over.

No. Thank you. No need. I'm fine.

I'm coming over, Paul said.

OK, Paul, Jane said.

As he drove to his mother-in-law's house to pick up his daughter, Robert thought of the only conversation he'd had with Pierce, the one at the Trolley. What they said to each other, what they talked about, he couldn't recall. Boxing? Did he give the kid advice? Did they discuss the fight? Did he tell him what he always told young fighters, that boxing was like life?

Were they drunk? Probably. Were they happy? Were they sad?
He didn't remember. What he remembered were the bruises on
the kid's face, his wet, red eyes. The kid dabbed at his eye with
a cocktail napkin to stop the leak. The rest was a blur.

Boxing is like life.

Hail Mary, full of grace.

Boxing *is* life. Sounded now like

The Lord is with thee.

bullshit.

And though he didn't remember the conversation and probably never would again, somewhere in Robert's brain, lost,
hidden beneath the bleeding and bruising and dead tissue
where what seemed like a lifetime of battles had taken their
toll, he knew the conversation remained, inaccessible, but
there all the same.

If it would only open up you could see inside...

He passed a grocery store, a fast-food place, a gas station. He
passed a market, a video store. When they were in his rearview
mirror, he looked back and did not remember their names.

And yet after all these years it had stayed with him: *Hail
Mary, full of grace, the Lord is with thee; blessed art thou
among women, and blessed is the fruit of thy womb, Jesus. Holy
Mary, Mother of God, pray for us sinners, now and at the hour
of our death. Amen.*

And he remembered: *Our Father, who art in heaven, hal-
lowed be Thy name, Thy Kingdom come, Thy will be done, on
earth as it is in heaven. Give us this day our daily bread, and forgive us our trespasses as we forgive those who trespass against
us, and lead us not into temptation, but deliver us from evil.
Amen.*

He pulled into his mother-in-law's driveway and honked the
horn. The front door opened and his daughter came running
out with her backpack. She ran awkwardly, her arms pumping
but the backpack weighing her down.

What did I tell you about that backpack? he said as she climbed up into the truck.

What?

It's too heavy. Leave some of that at school.

I need it.

You don't need it all. Not all of it.

The sign said one more mile to the border.

Good night, the bartender said, and Eric and Marty and Pete waved, said good night, and walked out the backdoor. It was cold outside, and dark. The clock on the bank across the street said ten-thirty. They were full now, bloated. Marty tripped on the gravel, tore his slacks. The other two picked him up. Ow, he said. Where to now? and Eric said,

Nowhere for me. Home. Work tomorrow.

Pete said to Marty, I'm game if you wanna go somewhere else.

Let's get a drink somewhere else, Marty said to Eric. He tugged on his arm. Come on, Chicken, just one more. One more toast to Jimmy the Kid.

Nah, I'm done. You guys go.

I'll go with you, Pete said and Marty said,

I guess I gotta work tomorrow too. I guess I'll go home, and Pete said,

Yeah. Let's just go home.

Then they got in their cars and drove away. In a few hours they would go to work.

Half a mile to the border.

Angela was asleep on the couch. Lying on her back, her neck bent against the armrest. One heel on the ground, one arm dangled over the side of the couch, fingers almost, but not quite, touching the carpet. The TV was on, showing a late movie, but the sound was off and there wasn't a light on in the house. Down the hall in the bedroom, the baby stood up in his crib, using the bars for balance, watching a multi-colored mobile spin above him, caught by a gust of wind from an open window. He watched the shapes spin, dim now, blue and gray in the mostly dark room; the only light, soft, faint, stretched in from the street, through the cracks between the blinds. He watched the shapes above him but did not try to touch them, having learned already the concept of reach, of distance, having learned that his arms were not long enough, that the shapes were too far away. He sat down with a thud, then rolled onto his back and watched them spin until he fell asleep and dreamt of them some more.

There were no other cars at the border and Bill pulled up to the painted line and stopped. Inside the booth two uniformed men were talking to each other. They looked out at him, and in no hurry, kept on with their conversation. It was raining. And the rain beat on the roof of the car. The windshield wipers whirred. Bill was tired. He felt that if he closed his eyes he might fall asleep.

The men laughed and one of them put on a raincoat and a plastic hat with a wide brim and came out of the booth. Bill rolled his window down.

How you doing tonight! the man shouted over the rain.

Fine!

What is your purpose for visiting Canada!

Bill didn't know. He hadn't planned on coming this far.

Your purpose? the man said.

I don't know! I should just turn around! I was out driving! I didn't mean to come this far!

The man nodded. He understood.

Follow me! he said, and he walked past the car and behind it, motioning Bill with his hand to back up as the rain pelted him, walking backwards, drawing a semi-circle in the air, showing Bill the way to turn around. Bill put the car in reverse and, looking behind him, slowly backed up, following the man, thirty feet or so behind the line, no-man's land. Rain blew in through the open window. The man stopped, finally, and motioned Bill to keep coming until he was even with him. He pointed left to a small thoroughfare that arced, splitting the grass meridian. Follow the arrows! he said, and waved Bill on. Bill followed the arrows on the road, followed them around the arc until he came to a booth on the other side. He stopped at a red light and another man came out, shouted over the rain.

Coming home? the man said.

Yeah!

How long you been gone!

What?

How long you been gone!

I never left!

How long have you been gone, sir!

I never left! I'm just turning around!

The man bent down and looked at Bill squarely, rain spilling off the brim of his hat.

You got ID? I'll need to see some ID!

Bill pulled his wallet out of his pocket, took his license out and handed it to the man. The man studied Bill's face, looked at the license, looked back at his face again.

Bill didn't say anything. He smiled.

The man handed him his license—Good night!—and waved him on.

Good night.

Bill rolled up his window, stepped on the gas and soon he was back on the other side again, headed south, building speed, each sign and marker he passed a reassurance that he had never left.

Good night, Robert said.

Good night.

He turned off Amy's light and closed the door, leaving it open a crack. Then he went into the bedroom. Ruth asleep, he moved the switch on the clock by the bed to wake him up at five, went into the bathroom, picked up a tube of Icy Hot from the counter, then back into the bedroom and turned off the light. The house was quiet. He walked down the hall, locked the front door, around to the kitchen, picked up a vial of Advil from the counter, made sure the sliding glass door was locked. It was. Then he went in and sat down on the couch, set the tube down, turned the TV on with the remote. He flipped through until he came to an old middleweight title fight from many years before.

The fight hadn't yet started and the cameras went back and forth to both corners, the fighters standing tall and calm as the trainers removed their robes. Robert knew who would win. He'd seen it a hundred times. He had it on tape. They stood, listening, nodding their heads, their eyes focused—one looked into the eyes of his trainer, the other into the distance—waiting for the fight to begin.

In the beginning, Robert had believed that he was going to do something special. He believed that someday he would be a main event, that he would make Ruth a million dollars, back then, in the beginning, when he was young and the dream was real and alive, when it seemed that every time he fought he won. And Ruth was always there. And when he'd win, he'd climb down through the ropes and she'd run up and throw her arms around him. They'd go home and he'd skip work the next day sometimes and they'd stay in bed, talking about their plans, the places they were going to go together, the things they were going to see and do. He imagined all the things he would buy for her.

But then he started losing. And he didn't understand why. He trained even harder, got in better shape. But his boxing wasn't getting better; he had no real technique, and the other fighters were figuring him out. He started losing more than he won and afterwards, when he'd lose, he'd climb down through the ropes, slowly, and Ruth would get up from her seat, slowly, and she'd put her purse over her shoulder and wait for him in the aisle. She'd take his hand and they'd walk out together, slowly. And he kept working on his technique but it never came and he kept losing and he couldn't stand anymore for her to see him lose, so one night in the truck on the way home he told her not to come anymore, he said he didn't want her there. He told her she was bad luck. They were still kids then. You're bad luck, he said, and she had cried. And she stopped coming and he told himself it would only be a little while, just until he got on track again, because surely this was only a dip in the road, he'd get on track again soon, and then she'd be back in the seats again, proud of him, rooting him on again. And he fought without her and he lost some and won some, and she would know by the expression on his face when he got home what had happened. And if he'd won she would ask him to tell her all about it, and he would, and if he'd lost, she wouldn't say a thing. But after awhile it didn't really matter anymore, he was getting tired and even winning wasn't exciting anymore—it wasn't enough just to win— because nothing was happening; his record was bad, he wasn't moving up, nobody was calling; he was realizing he wasn't good enough. But he still fought because he'd had a dream and now he was awake but he couldn't forget the dream.

And life went on. He took time off now and then, a few months here and there, then back into training and the ring. He got jobs and lost them, he found new jobs. He fought and won and lost. And Ruth got pregnant. And he lost more fights. And he won some and it didn't matter and by now he was too old to be fighting these boys, anyway, it was an embarrassment, but he kept fighting, never getting better, never moving up, no one interested in him. And she had the baby. And somewhere along the way his brain started closing up on itself. He started forgetting things. And his head was hurting so much all the time, and Ruth said it was time to quit, and he looked for new trainers because they kept quitting on him, but Robert didn't quit. And his hands and his joints ached, and his head hurt so much, and there was always so much pain, and Ruth said it was time to quit but he didn't quit, he kept fighting, and there was always so much pain and he kept forgetting things, things he knew he should remember—he forgot his anniversary, he forgot Amy's birthday, he'd forget what day it was, he'd forget what month it was, he'd forget sometimes, only for a moment, that he had a wife and a daughter, that he had anyone at all. And finally he began to forget what it felt like to believe and Ruth said it was time to quit, and now he had finally forgotten the dream, because he no longer remembered believing, and he promised her that this one would be his last. And he fought. He put everything he had on it. And he lost.

Glory be to the Father, and to the Son, and to the Holy Spirit. As it was in the beginning, is now, and always shall be. Amen.

The bell rang. The fighters on the TV screen left their corners and walked out to the center of the ring. They met and began to circle each other, their hands up, bobbing, moving, and he remembered:

Stick him with your right.

Stick him with your right.

Step in. Jab.

Back him up.

Wait for it…

Wait for that opening…

Wait for your opening...

His head hurt. Robert opened the vial and shook out a few pills into the palm of his hand, tilted his head back, dropped them in, left them sitting on his tongue until he had enough saliva to swallow them down, then swallowed. He picked up the tube next. He squirted some paste onto the back of his hand, set the tube down, and massaged the paste in and around his knuckles, around his wrists, rubbed his palms with his thumbs. He looked up at the TV—

—a quick left jab followed by a hard right hook that the other fighter blocked easily. Then the two began trading blows, missing with most, blocking what they could, stepping in, falling back, and again. It would go on like this until the end.

He wiped his hands on his shorts, reached for his pack and took out a cigarette. Couldn't find the matches. Where had he put them?

Not on the coffee table. Not on the carpet. Hadn't fallen below the chair...

Here they are.

Robert took the book out of his pocket and struck a match. Lit his cigarette and set the match in the ashtray. He watched the flame grow as it traveled down the matchstick, orange at the center surrounded by a soft blue sheath. Watched it grow, and the embers glow behind the flame, then the center began to shrink, fade, and finally, it disappeared.

He'd watch the first few rounds. He'd watch the first few and call it a night.

It's going to be all right, Tom said.

They were back now. The lights were off and it was pitch black in the room. Tom could feel the blanket tighten around him as Anna moved her legs. She sighed. The shot the doctor had given her had taken effect and her nose didn't hurt anymore, what she felt was a tightness in her face, she felt she was made of water everywhere else. She breathed through her mouth.

It wasn't broken, just badly bruised. You need to take it easy for awhile, the doctor had said. You're exhausted, and he had taken Tom into the hall and Anna had stayed there, on the uncomfortable hospital bed, she felt sleepy, it must be the shot, she thought, I'm so tired, it must be the shot, closed her eyes. Tom carrying her, setting her in the car, she fell asleep, reaching for the small, bright circle so far away. Tom undressing her, putting her in bed, then she had watched his blurry shape undress, walk to the light switch, turn out the lights, felt him crawl in beside her. She was filled to the brim—filled to the brim—she always cried in churches—always did—she didn't know why...

It's going to be all right.

And Tom was afraid. In the dark, in the stillness, he was afraid. He felt the blanket tighten around him as Anna moved and sighed and he was afraid.

He would get up in the morning. He would make sure she was comfortable, he would give her some pills if she were to wake, some pills to set her asleep again, when she was asleep he would go downstairs and catch up on his paperwork. He would come up every few minutes to check on her.

How long this day had been. That a single day could take so long...

Tom lay in the dark. He thought of his brother. He wondered what it had been like for Jimmy at the end.

Was there a song playing on the radio? Was there noise from out on the street? Could he hear the voices of people in other rooms? Could he hear through the walls? Could he understand what they were saying?

What was the last thing he remembered? What was the last thing he felt? Who was the last person he thought about?

WAS IT DARK LIKE THIS?

Did he see a light?

Did it open up?

Did it usher him in?

I'm sorry, Anna said. I need— and she began to cry, softly.
It's going to be all right, Tom said.

It's fine now.

It's going to be

fine.

Outside, someone started a car. Backed up and stopped. Moved into first gear. Drove on, shifted, and disappeared down the street.

Tom reached out and put his hand on Anna's thigh. She felt his hand on her thigh.

ALL IS WELL

When the season was over and the boat came back to Seattle, the first thing James always did was to go down to the Pioneer Square Saloon and see if he could find any of his friends. Sometimes they were there and scoring was no problem. Sometimes he had to foot-it all around the city with his pack over his shoulder, looking. Usually he rented a cheap room with a bed and a sink, but sometimes, if it wasn't too late and he wanted to save money for a night or two, he went down to the mission. He liked hanging out in bars with people and sharing his dope with them. Sometimes it was old retired guys and most of them only liked to drink. Sometimes it was people he knew from the old days and most of them had stopped all that nonsense, told him he should cut it out too. Often he'd find companionship with the white kids who'd hang around the bars downtown, and they'd always smoke with him, sometimes come around a few days later looking for him. James never forgot a name and he liked to be close to people when he talked to them. He felt good giving these kids advice about life. A lot of them didn't have father figures and he liked to think of himself as a father figure. Sometimes he would invite these kids back to his room to hang out and talk, but they would never have the time. So he'd give them a folded-up piece of tin foil and a tube and let them have a smoke, then maybe play a game of pool. Maybe they'd buy him a drink. He'd take the drink but it was the only sort of payment he would take. He never sold to them or made them pay for what he gave. That would be against the spirit. When they'd come back looking for him he'd call them by name, laugh, and yell at the bartender to bring his young friends some drinks. He'd put his arms around them and tell them they better be staying out of trouble. It made him feel good when people came looking for him. Back in the day he had been a trumpet player in a funk band and everyone was always looking for him. He was well-known around town those days and he had a yellow Cadillac convertible that he drove all around. That car was the envy of the entire scene. Sometimes on nice days he would drive around with his wife and his baby, the top down, cool wind rushing around their heads. Now his wife and daughter were back down in Federal Way living with a man, and James had a picture of his daughter sitting sideways on a football field with one leg raised in a triangle and her chin resting on her knee. She was wearing a sweatshirt that said *Decatur High* and her hair was cut short. She had beautiful brown eyes and skin. Everyone he showed the picture to said how beautiful she was and he'd tell them she was the spitting image of her mother at that age, all eyes and legs and he would laugh.

There were some bartenders who didn't want to see him anymore so he avoided those bars, and there were some old friends who didn't want to see him anymore and had never been happy to see him. He had done bad and stupid things to people in the old days and he felt terrible about it. One of these people was his wife. He had never been good to his wife and she had a legitimate beef about a lot of things. One of the first things he always did after the boat came back to Seattle was mail a letter to his wife with some money in it. He'd write her a long letter and tell her jokes in the letter and reminisce and ask if she remembered the good times and at the end of each letter he would ask her to send him a picture of their daughter and he would always hint that he'd like to come for dinner or for a weekend here or there, but with the picture she'd send him each year, there would never be an invitation.

The last time James ever came back from the boat he bought some heroin and went to the Saloon where he met a kid in a sports jacket. He talked to the kid for a long time and they had drinks and shots of tequila and the kid said, They lose tonight they won't make the playoffs, and James said, Is that so? I had no idea. It's been so long since I kept up, and he showed his tube to the kid and told him he could go ahead and have a smoke if he wanted. The kid stood up, and walked into the other room where the bar was. James went into the bathroom and smoked some of the heroin and washed his face and when he came back out the bartender was clearing James' glass off the counter and he told James to get out, he told him he'd been warned before, he told him not to come back, and as James was walking out with his pack, he saw the kid in the sports jacket sitting at the bar, staring up at the ballgame on the television. James was high and very drunk and he stumbled out the door. It was raining hard and he walked down an alley and ducked into a doorway. He hadn't found a place to sleep for the night yet and he sat on the ground and didn't want to ever move again, but after a few minutes in the cold, he took his pack and walked down to the mission where he got in line. He ate his dinner and talked to the men around him. He stayed awake for a long time down in the basement, talking in the dark to the man on the cot next to his, an Indian with a swollen red face named Ralph. Ralph listened to James talk about his daughter and life on the boat and the kid he'd met in the Saloon earlier and all the kids who used to come and hang out with him.

Ralph listened to James talk about his Cadillac and trumpeters he'd played with and his funk band and those long drives. James liked talking to Ralph remembering these things and they held the foil for each other, blowing the sweet smoke into their blankets. Ralph listened for a long time and said he hated every fucking white man he'd ever met, and James told him, Now, people were people and it's not the color of a man that counts, but what's inside. He'd learned that over the years and Ralph listened, staring at the ceiling, and seemed hip to it. James dug Ralph. He loved him. Ralph was cool. Ralph was the type of guy who would never let another guy down. It was wonderful how cool people could be.

9/03

STAY CALM EVERYTHING WILL BE OK
WE ARE HERE TO HELP YOU